THE BIRTH OF A STORY

Books by William Sansom

The Birth of a Story

WILLIAM SANSOM

1972

CHATTO & WINDUS ✦ THE HOGARTH PRESS

LONDON

Published by
Chatto & Windus Ltd and The Hogarth Press Ltd
42 William IV Street, London W.C.2
*
Clarke, Irwin and Company Ltd
Toronto

NET 7012 0370 6

NON NET 7010 0487 8

Printed Offset Litho in Great Britain
by Cox & Wyman Ltd,
London, Fakenham and Reading

75472

Contents

1

In Case of Interest

A word about the reason for this book. The photographed reproduction of manuscripts in critical studies of an author's work are usually those of dead authors. The crossings out and the additions of these dead men are there for all to see and to try to understand, and the living critic helps this along with a text of his own. But he points out only his own idea of the reasons for these corrections. His are perhaps clever guesses, but they are nevertheless guesses. The reader is at liberty to guess otherwise. In all this, the only silent figure is the one who had no need to guess — the horse's mouth, the author.

So it occured to me that it might be of interest if a living author himself described, to his best ability, the reasons for correcting this or that in a manuscript, so to bring the reader close in to a writer's daily problems of technique. Since at the time of writing I am still alive, I could do this. Moreover, the idea could be broadened to describe the whole process of attempting a literary work, from its initial germ as an idea to its finished form for publication. And this could be treated not so much in the usual remote terms of critical analysis, but more in the close manner of a seminar, questioning myself and answering as I go along.

Such an *exposé*, I thought, had better be about a short work of some kind. As a writer of short stories I seemed to be in a good position to do this. A short story seemed to be an ideal subject, long enough to invite solid consideration, short enough to be reasonably digestible.

Here, then, is such a story along with pages of its manuscript and typescript, and with my own detailed commentary: *No Smoking on the Apron*. It is, of course, a personal approach. Other writers may have entirely different methods of work. This is only how one particular writer went to work. In passing, that will be the reason for the frequent intrusion into this text of a big little word difficult to handle, I, for which I now apologize. The first person all too easily sounds immodest.

It implies the beamish boy. I do not mean it so: this book is not about quality, but about how, personally, one author goes about things. A kind of peep-show, in case of interest.

2
Writing a Short Story

1. *Why?* In the first place, why write a story at all?

Broadly, because to tell a story is an impulse as old as the bards and whoever preceded them. The hairy men with harps recited their sagas thousands of years ago, the storytellers in today's Arab markets still command an audience, money, entrancement. We ourselves, in our daily lives, give and take the drama of the day — we are forever telling each other stories of what happened round the corner last Wednesday. The impulse is as plain as a pikestaff, whatever that is; but in daily use it is a muddy pikestaff, and it is the professional writer's task or pleasure to pan that mud for its gold dust.

From time to time there rises the howl: 'The Novel is dead!' 'The Short Story is dead!'. This is nonsense. The form is being constantly modulated, but the narrative essence continues strong. Today there is less chance of that essence dying than of the disappearance of today's material means of communicating it, word and page. The far future hints that books may be replaced by projected microfilms; or audio-books of words, or of an actor reading words, or even of the whole thing being treated in dramatic form on micro-television. If it happens, it will be regrettable. Gone will be the luxury of turning back to dwell on this or that passage. Gone also the shape and spelling of words, aesthetic pleasures in themselves. And with the third alternative, tele-drama, we will be faced with all the serious limitations of television drama as we know it today. Gone also will be the flow of imagination in the mind of the reader — home-*cinéaste* in the studio of his own skull.

Until all this happens stories will go on being written. Even if the first outlets, magazines and newspapers, serve them not so well, they will nevertheless be written because writers like to write them. As with poetry, much of which never sees the light of a reader's eye.

2. *How?*   And how to write a story?

There are no set rules. Like the novel, the short story is elastic in form. Broadly, the novel relates the interplay of a number of characters, whereas the short story is concerned with one episode or tendency in the lives of one or two people. The short story is really nearer to a poem than its apparent prose-brother, the novel. It is usually about one thing, blown up big or refined beneath the microscope. It can take the form of a moody piece occurring in one person's mind, or a stream of consciousness in the author's mind, or a classic narrative with a beginning, a middle and an end: to adopt this latter technique, it does not follow that the story is old fashioned, it can taste as fresh as tomorrow.

Similarly the plot or narrative of a story can be made to seem as fresh as next Tuesday, though it will probably be as old as the hills: we have often heard that there are only so and so many plots in the world, and this is true, though it is equally true that their possibilities of permutation are endless. The success of a story is never so much what it is about as how it is told: what persons and scenes are projected, with what subtlety or force they are handled, and how the words themselves are chosen. This choice of words and their composite cadence is naturally the test of a good or bad writer. Whatever the style chosen, as toughly economic as Hemingway's, as involuted as Henry James's, as intentionally loose as Radiguet's, there are assonances for the inner ear of the speaking mind which, among much else, make or break prose. A simple, but always astonishing test of this is to compare a good and bad translation of a foreign work: here, line by line, is the same literal meaning phrased by a good and a bad ear. One can learn a lot from this. Or -- can one learn at all how to be a 'good' user of words? Passable, yes. But good? I suspect that the ability is a gift, inborn or conditioned pretty early on – the result of an ear naturally disposed towards the music of words, to the music of spelling even, and to an involvement with the usage of words well beyond that of a normal person: not at this stage hard work at all, a natural bent, a pleasure.

To tell a story implies plainly a narrative ability. How to intersperse description with action, and in what quantities? How much to dwell on the minor activities of a character, which will reveal that character, before continuing the major action of the drama itself? How much dialogue? How much straight statement, how much silent implication of the underlying theme? And so on. All these quantities will depend on nothing but the quality of the author's taste, and on his response to certain undeniable influences of life outside literature.

I mean technical influences, like, say, the cinema. Add now television and the increase of the photographed image in newspapers, magazines. In short, the new great currency of the Image. Whether this enormous pictorial increase makes us see more clearly is debatable: it is possible that too quick a succession of images becomes blurred, cancels itself out, as with the pictures in an art gallery when one tries to see too much in too short a visit; it is possible that a Victorian faced with a few oleographs absorbed much more (compare the lasting impression of the illustrations in a book read and prized in childhood). But what is certain is that the frequency of the image projected at us has resulted in an increase of movement or action. Even a motionless photographed figure, static in itself, implies action before and afterwards. And certainly in films or television you cannot have a figure on the screen sitting about and doing nothing for long.

This has had its effect on writing. The pace has increased. It would have increased in any case, through the cutting away of the worst verbiage of the past, when manners were slower and to our present perceptions tediously involved. We are, at least superficially, quicker in everything. But the film, I think, has had a deeper effect on fiction than anything else. Usually, the words 'film' and 'literary man' used in the same breath invite suspicion: this is because many writers, particularly novelists, have debased their work by writing 'with an eye to film' — a bad habit, usually disastrous, a thoroughly self-conscious money-grubbing, and not worth discussing. I am talking of something quite different: of the aesthetic effects of the cinema on the mind of an author. For instance, the all-seeing godlike camera eye has whisked away the last need for the presence in a story of a narrator, of the eyes of one credible human being with whom you may identify your own, and through *only* which you may see the action of the story. The camera, popping about everywhere, has dispensed with the need for this. Brainwashed in the huge dark dreamlike cinema, the bookwriter follows suit. The presence of a narrator may still have a place; but he is no longer usually a necessity.

Similarly, the story-writer has been affected by the pace of action in the cinema. Unconsciously he has copied the restless camera and moved his prose at a faster pace: the visualizing element just behind the bone of his forehead is itself a kind of cinema screen, and easily infected. It is infected by the worst, but also by the best — that is his choice as an artist.

Again, dialogue will have altered. There will not necessarily be less of it, but what there is will line by line be foreshortened. The author will feel the greater presence of the image which shortens dialogue on the screen itself with the help of facial expressions, thinnings of lips, rollings of eyes — and expect his readers to feel it too. A reasonable assumption, since they have been to the cinema too and are themselves part of this faster pace.

From this it may be feared that certain subtleties will suffer. The story-writer's one great plus over the other arts has hitherto been an ability to enter a character's mind and describe what goes on there. On the screen this can only be implied, by expression or action. It may be that now the story-writer also feels he must imply rather than state. In small doses, this has, I think always been a virtue in a writer: it is the subtler way to guide the reader's feelings into subtlety. But it can be taken too far: the writer can be un-nerved, and cut everything of the unspoken inside in favour of the spoken appearance.

This is a pity, because it is not compensated for by being able to borrow in return several natural advantages the visual arts have always had over the written word. For one, portraiture of the human face: this is at best only clumsily possible on the written page. For another, intonations of speech: the writer can rely only on clichés like 'he said softly' or 'her voice rose' or the occasional word italicized for emphasis — none of which will approach the complex subtleties of the spoken voice itself.

Once again the solutions lie in the taste of the individual author. He is a unique computer fed by experience and sensual choice, what goes in will be smoothly docketed, whirled, and come clicking out in a unique message. This unique message he will then correct and mould according to his again unique critical faculty. But here comes a rub — for how long should he go on correcting, re-moulding? Correction is of course vital. But it can become over-nervous. Leave a painter with a painting exposed in his studio for months and he will always be at it. The same with a writer and his text. He becomes over-involved, judge-, ment goes.

In this, I myself have had two lessons which I have never forgotten. One was when I was writing copy in an advertising agency. Copy is usually of a most economic nature — every word is calculated to count, space is money. So one wrote and chiselled, and came up finally with something which seemed excitingly perfect for the purpose. But a month or so later that same advertisement was scheduled for publicat-ion in a provincial paper allowing only half the original space for words. So out came the chisel again and a word here was lopped, another there. Astonishing result — it seemed as good, often better than the original. This experience has left me with a hard attitude towards my own prose, a stronger wish to root out double and triple epithets, a readier blue pencil for beloved purple words. Healthy; but like most medicines a danger if applied too ruthlessly.

The second lesson I learned was from an older and established writer whose work I admired. He took a page of mine published in a magazine and said: 'Now let's cut out all the unnecessary words', and went at it with a pencil. He got out a very great deal. I was surprised, secretly mortified. But he was undeniably right. The page was full of what painters call spinach. Those disastrous double epithets when one, more carefully chosen, would have done the job. Unnecessary 'howevers' and 'buts', my own breath longer than the putative reader's. The result was an improvement, and a right rap over the knuckles for the purple passage. Good advice, in fact, but again not without its dangers. Certain internal rhythms were lost, there was a sensation now too stark. The answer to all this is again only taste, qualitative, quantitive, and, if possible for one so personally involved, a clear and clinical mind. Perhaps the best technical way out of such a dilemma is to put the manuscript in a drawer for three months, and come to it again as another person. But this brings up a further problem:

3. *For Whom*? For whom do you write a story?

Two opposing camps here. One says, write entirely for yourself, with thoughts of publication secondary, a pleasant consequence. The other says, write for a large audience, with publication well in mind. (Publication in either case follows; what I mean is the motive behind the writing: what kind of reader have you in mind?)

I belong near to camp one. I write for myself and a projection of myself, a tyrannical oligarchy of a dozen or more editors, distant schoolmasters, and literate friends whose taste I respect. With these in mind, the words come out with mixed feelings of discretion and rebellion: I fear my masters a bit, and at the same time I want to cock a snook at them.

This imaginary readership of an elect few does not mean that the work shall be over-intellectualized, full of five-syllable words and arcane references, so oblique as to be obscure. I deplore obscurity, and, although suffering from the writer's purple disease, try hard — and it is hard — to be as sparing and taut with words as I can; yet without sounding 'tough', or talking rather than writing. In the last few decades there has been a growing disposition for writers to write in a talkative way. It is thought to be frank, intimate, unassuming. The result is too often simply cheap. In the hands of a really good writer, like Salinger in *The Catcher in the Rye*, it comes off splendidly: but, like Hemingway with his deceptive simplicity, it is not only talk but double and treble talk, a lot of work or intuition has gone into formalizing an apparently straight monologue. My firm belief is that one should not write as one talks, but write as one would wish to talk given the time, trouble and fearlessness to do so. Nothing overdone, but equally nothing underdone. (In all this, I refer of course to the prose outside actual dialogue. The story or novel written entirely in dialogue is its own excuse.)

My own wedding with a chosen few readers (who are, of course, multiplied thousands of times by similar readers I do not know) began suddenly, and so factually as to be worth re-telling. It happened during the Hitler war. Before that war, I had worked for an advertising agency, grading from the copy department to the music and drama side producing programmes for radio. I had a good executive position, directed daily many of the best musicians and actors of the day, and thought I knew everything. In fact, we did know a lot: we knew what the public wanted, and, more expertly, what the public were likely to want in six months' time. But, of course, only in that particular medium. Innocently and indulgently, I imagined I knew what the public would want in other media too, for instance in the province of the short story. In the evenings I wrote piles of short stories with 'magazine formulas' in mind. They were all returned. Over several years and with no exception.

With the war, I left the agency and joined the Fire Brigade. When the blitz began, after a night or two in London's docks, we were all convinced we would be dead in a week. We worked in shifts, forty-eight hours on, twenty-four off. On one of these off-days I thought, Hell I'll write down exactly what all this feels like. In view of my coming decease, I was then in no way concerned with possible publication. I simply wanted to put down the truth for myself.

This I did, in a short fire-fighting episode called *The Wall*. Meanwhile the bombing continued, and against all prediction, we were not all killed. So there was this manuscript to hand, and months later, quite by chance, a friend of a friend picked it up and took it along to the offices of Cyril Connolly's monthly *Horizon*. This intermediary was not even on the editorial side of the magazine. And I myself would never, never have thought of submitting the MS to so very august a body (I had no literary pretentions, thought *Horizon* and such far above me). So the whole matter was a considerable fluke. But the episode or story was instantly accepted.

And when it was published, real live publishers came on the telephone to me asking for a book. In a word, the little piece was an overnight success, and its reception set me off writing like a racing engine.

Naturally, by now I had reflected on why *The Wall* had worked, and concluded, I think rightly, that it was because it was not calculated to please people, but to please the truth. So I went on writing what I wanted truthfully to write, and pretty well everything thenceforth was accepted by the literally media of those days, *Penguin New Writing, Life and Letters, English Story, The Cornhill* and others.

The truth, the wish to tell it to myself and a few others, was plainly the kernel of the matter. Of course, style came into it too. This one can attribute mostly to a personal ear for words, and to selected reading: though again, I think, a desire for true statement has its effect on style. The atmosphere is opposed to tricks, affectation, calculation.

In those early days, critics were quick to see the influence of Kafka in my work. How then could these fantasies be aligned with the truth, which usually implies realism? But Kafka himself based all his fantasies on his own experience of the Bohemian and Austrian bureaucracy and what it did to his paranoiac self: and he kept his fables, as is vital with fantasy, with their feet close to the ground. Realism, in fact, of a different kind.

In passing, what I appreciated most in Kafka were matters like his description of, say, a room — free from all unnecessary detail, but dead solid on where the windows are, the steps, the door, giving you an absolute sense of thereness: and I liked the shadowy initial, with neither a name nor an exact personality, for his central character, with whose ominous neutrality you can the more forcibly identify yourself. Kafka's work is of permanent value; and one permanent quality is that he never explained but left questions implicit. My own Kafkaesque works were well received, but I think failed, because at that time I was a youngish man ripe for vehement philosophizing and putting the world right, and I did not leave things implicit, I explained and stated. Heavy handed. Then of course one must remember that Kafka could not have been my only influence. I can well remember what no critic could notice, my intense interest in the Rilke of *Malte Laurids Brigge* and, particularly, in the meticulous eye of François Ponge. A hundred unremembered but formative others must be added.

A writer is also formed by his own life outside literature. A gregarious writer may find it easy and natural to recreate the nuances of social behaviour. A solitary may not do this so well, working from an experience of dislike if not hate, with a one-sided result; he will no doubt be better on weather and landscape. There are also axes to grind, and chips on shoulders: but here tread carefully, there is a world of difference between the heavy sermon and the inspired diatribe, between those two apparent twins of different fathers, earnestness and enthusiasm. We come here to the perpetual question of the 'engaged' writer — should one be so or not? I have always thought this to be in fact no question at all. There has never been a writer of any importance who is not 'engaged'. The question is only, 'engaged' with what? The problems of your particular decade, in a particular part of the world? Or the problems and study of human behaviour as a whole? The proper study of mankind is man. So it is, this way or that, in literature: with occasional offshoots, like otters and salmon.

My own make-up, for instance, is vitiated by being a painter *manqué*, a musician *manqué*, a dramatist *manqué* and a poet *manqué*. From early childhood, I have had a facility for drawing, a very 'visual' eye. In adolescence, my ambition, and practice, was to compose music. I also wrote poetry. Then there was the theatre calling, a light stench of greasepaint on the air. But at the same time, I had a pocket *manqué*, and had to earn a living. The arts, from my parents' standpoint, were too tricky. I did not rebel against their advice, but went into a bank; and four years later, because of that niggling aptitude with the pen, out of that and into an advertising agency. On the side, I composed and painted and wrote — all with vague ideas of professional sales, but impelled more by a dilettante facility and pleasure.

It was finally the war which decided me to concentrate any spare time on writing. There was a strong material consideration — all you needed was a pencil and paper and a quiet corner. I had already learned that with music you had to be a salesman too, hang around, make contracts, even perform your stuff: I was bad at all this. With painting, it is usually necessary to devote some considerable time to practical study, art school in fact, before you are truly in command of your materials and, say, the involved physiology of the human body. All this takes time. And time, if you also wanted to see a bit of life, there was not enough of. However, isolated in the monasterial seclusion of a fire station during lull periods, there was time indeed: not so easy to come by the materials for music or painting, but pencils and paper were to hand and, for the determined, quiet corners away from the fleshpots of ping-pong and darts.

Thus, for me, it all began: and for some reason, I think sometimes from selfconsciousness, from a nervousness of all that whiteness round the words, I gave up writing poetry. But the point of all this is that the influences of music, painting and poetry continue within the written work. Unconsciously, of course: but over the years now consciously too, in that when writing a story I like to see that all the senses are involved, sound, sight, smell, touch, taste plus such ancillary divisions as colour and, where apposite, a reference to an evocative piece of music. Here the only trouble I come up against is with words — the poetry: it comes readily — but how to merge it with a desired down-to-earth, economic prose? I pass that one to you.

4. *What?*   Questions of how, of form, bring us to questions of content — what to write a story about?

Of course, pretty well anything.

But let it, I think, be within the scope of the writer's own experience. This is not to say about himself, but about something he has himself experienced, perhaps only in a slight way, but nevertheless in a manner memorable enough to be safely exaggerated into a credible major experience. Also, characters and places and words known in actual life are the more visible and securely audible in the mind's eye and ear: their very solidity can also bring a chain reaction of forgotten memories, ready-made atmospheres and details which can then be safely adapted to the fiction involved. I have repeated 'safely', 'securely'; this, because a known thing has real presence — all-important, unanalysable details such as a torn shoe-lace or a special hair-colouring insert themselves with a mythical intensity — and also because the writer avoids factual mistakes, like the placing of dark granite in a similarly dark Italian tufa region, or the excrescence of impossible vegetations, or the mention, say, of 'coppers' in a uniquely brass and silver coinage. Little matters, but trip-ropes all — like beef in shepherd's pie, a patent impossibility, or putting anything else but walnut oil in a salad in the Perigord region. It can be and has been done carefully and successfully from imagination; but rarely outside the sphere of historical romance. One's own secure experience, sensually perceived, is the safe way; and this applies also to the people in stories, not necessarily pictures of particular acquaintances — dangerous! — but the mixing of those acquaintances with others of their type to make a credible amalgam.

Once or twice seen people in a bus or a pub — these are usually my own models. Friends are so close as to be invisible; or possibly with them one is too active, defensive and offensive, and thus unreceptive. Better if one is alone, on the watch, at a moment when the visionary juices are running. That is the time for a momentary but ineradicable picture. Provided that the figure you see, and the landscape into which you put it, are scored deeply enough in the memory, they should take on a life of their own, with all their chain reaction of smells and colour, music and kinds of motion, to be gently guided by the writer along the intended channels of his theme and, at best, to become so alive that they themselves take over, and apparently write the story for you.

This is a most mysterious and blessed event. Very often, on the best days, I have started work with only a vague outline in mind, yet by the end of the morning pages are filled with matters I never intended nor even knew I knew of. Something from outside me, or inside the characters, has been at work: I feel my own self to be no more than a portly penpushing catalyst, a kind of medium at the desk. Into the pages have strolled dogs never consciously conceived, ready-dressed strangers with pertinent remarks, ominous shopkeepers, touching tram-drivers, and a host of other chain reaction details all set in motion by the very reality of the main character. Obviously they come from my own forgotten experience, or they were inventions based on experience: but they would never, never have been dredged up without the vital influence of that first solid figure beginning to live in the cinema of the mind.

Such a character will see to his own development. For develop, or change direction, or show unexpected facets in his personality, a character must. In the same way he is usually the better for not being too much of a piece, being rounded in the manner of every human being, faults and good qualities interlarded. A too well-known, over-used example of a round character is the murderer who strokes pussy-cats. Such clichés must be freshened up: and this process of freshening, as with the composition of the prose itself, is the hard work.

To make our over-used language read as if under-used — yet without showing it — is, for me at least, the main and conscious struggle. A labour of love indeed, for what percentage of final readers will notice it? The little elect, as usual. Though in fact nobody should actively *notice* it: they should only notice that it is without cliché, that it is pure and good.

The same applies to your characters and your background — and the only way to know what will be recognized as old hat is to know what has been written before, is to read and read and read. This is where the writer of riper age usually scores, provided he is not stuck in the rut of his own earlier years. More time to have read more, more time to have thought more, more time to have experienced more. Though he had better keep himself interested and forward-looking, contain his middle-aged malaise for status quo and past. What has or has not 'been done before' is forever a bedevilling question: there is some quite arbitrary time factor abroad, characters and plots can become acceptable again, skip a generation or two, in the same way as fashion repeats itself after a period of being passé not past.

In passing, I may mention an occasional pitfall in reading. This occurs, infrequently, when the subject matter of some episode in a book becomes confused with one's own experience or imagination. And you write it as though created for the first time. I can give you an example. A number of years ago I was in the Pitti Palace in Florence. Sliding about before a quattrocento this, a cinquecento that — I soon realized the floors were very highly polished. And suddenly it struck me that these polished floors, the endless vistas of rooms and corridors, were better suited to roller skating than looking at pictures. So I wrote a story about a boy loose in the Pitti Palace on roller skates.

More recently, on a visit to Rome, sliding about in another such vast empty museum-palace, I was told that in Edwardian days a giddy Roman high society used in fact to roller skate in their palaces, the ladies in hats high with birds and berries, the gentlemen figuring with hands behind back. When they went out to dine, they took their boots and skates in a bag, tiaras and all. Now — I find that at least three authors have written of this. I myself have no recollection whatsoever of reading any of these three authors. I could swear that such roller skating was an ordinary sensuous thought which might occur to any-one — and it occurred thus to me. (After all, it occurred to those Romans.) But can I be sure? Can I be sure I didn't read it? I can swear myself black and blue in the face and not be sure.

No story is new, only its ingredients; and those ingredients had best be taken from life, not books. The writer must be observer and public detective. But here a curious dichotomy arises, for he must observe both clinically and with engaged emotion. He must have this dual but conflicting ability in his chemical make-up.

He must also deal with a coming and going of his ability to observe. Some days, everything looks dull; but on others the most ordinary matters of life take on a wild visionary significance — simple things, the glove dropped in the gutter, the way a hand poses a cigarette, the kind of smile a smile is, a weed, a postman, a crane. All such things, on the good days, become suddenly and deeply perceived by the artist. A kind of inbuilt mescalin takes over inside him, he is most actively entranced by the appearance and meaning of things. This is a gift. It can perhaps be trained, or cultivated, or at least watched so that nothing — like a social obligation — comes in the way of it. The loose word for it is inspiration, but that word hardly describes the extra-ordinary passion, and, better, compassion, of these bright and powerful moments of controlled delirium.

I wrote above that a story can be about anything. That goes. But whether it is acceptable by a large public is another matter. There is the sad truth that man is still largely nine-tenths animal. Thus, sex and violence can be the easiest ways into him. I have noticed, with stories of mine which have been more than usually reprinted, that these have contained elements of sex or violence, and have been read at a very different level to what I intended: the profounder underlying themes have been ignored for the superficially excitant veneer. With the greater use of the pictured image in our lives, sex and violence have become obsessional. Now it is becoming unusual to pick up a novel without coming across some set sex scene. Very well, people go to bed with each other. But it seems to me dull, dull to try to describe in intimate detail what they do with each other there. It is like describing eating, or some involved meal. And even Petronius Arbiter grows dull as he wades through Trimalchio's feast. No, sex is only interesting, like anything else, in as much as it illuminates life. That a television supper is burning in the oven while the lovers are in bed is of far more interest than the moods of their genitalia; let the oven catch fire, and life and the kitchen are illumined indeed. It is *thought*, motive, reason that matter; sex times why equals head.

For by all that is wonderful, keener human feelings do still obtrude. Romantic love, if brought reasonably up-to-date, can still win. As can also other pulls on the fine emotions — pity, compassion, kindness, the unforeseen act which jerks tears. When the baddie suddenly turns kind and good — this is a famous moment which seldom fails. Such gambits are equally the ploy of bad and good writers — it is once again the 'how it is done', the taste and tact and wisdom and feeling of the writer which makes literature or does not. One is much in the situation of a divine plumber in charge of a godhead sluice — loosing it and damming it as the supply of action, character, description, heat and cold seem instinctively right. Yet, with the best of artistry taken for granted, it would seem sometimes that it is a robust content which makes a story live on and on. There are obvious cases — like Maupassant's human and harrowing *The Necklace*, so constantly reprinted while much of his subtler work is forgotten. Like W.W. Jacob's *The Monkey's Paw*. But then . . . is this really so? Chekhov's wonderful *Lady with the Toy Dog* is about — what? A man falling in love with a married woman, and their patient realization of a hopeless future. And Thomas Mann's *Death in Venice?* Little action but the slow brooding of death, the search in the mind for lost youth, the decay of moral resolution. So — there are no rules. Except to write about what has moved you, and to write it well.

A question often asked is what sets an author off on a story. Is it a very conscious process: 'I will write a story about greed', and thence the arbitrary selection of characters and background and action? Or is it an inspirational moment — a sudden vision of an act of greed, and a furbishing of a story round this, giving it a beginning and an end? Or is it a wish to write about a certain person in mind — and a moment of greed is taken arbitrarily as the action? The written work cannot give an answer to this question; and the author is unavailable for questioning. Once again, I can only speak for myself. With me, the fruition of an idea is usually gradual, and comes from different directions.

Broadly, I sometimes look at my own experience of life and think: I have known this large emotion, that base fear, this sense of envy, and so on. All are subjects I would like to express in a story. Then round about that time, or even years earlier, I would have been most impressed by a certain landscape, or house, or room — angles of its light, grades of its colour, essences of its smell, altogether its sensuous presence: and the mind's notebook will have it engraved for future use somewhere, at some time. Then comes one of those days of visionary excitation — I see, perhaps in a bus, perhaps on a station platform, some small or large human action which suddenly seems extraordinarily, deliriously significant.

The whole matter now consolidates. That small action seen seems to pull from nowhere the first two elements of theme and background: they have, with many others, been lying dormant for months, years — yet they are suddenly and clearly remembered and, what seems to me so extraordinary, declare themselves as the only theme and background possible for the illumination of this action. And either the person actually seen involved in that action, or some modulation of that type of person, or even someone else filed in the memory — any of these three abruptly sets solid and immovable on the now illuminated mental screen, and the story comes into being, seems from then on to tell itself.

An instance: I well remember the genesis of a story of mine *The Vertical Ladder*, in its essence an essay on vertigo, whose constant anthologizing seems to have proved its success. It began, vaguely, when I was a fireman. There were all those ladders to climb, and I suffered miseries of vertigo — not at night in action, when such fears were blurred by other excitements, but in the cold light of day and the training yard. Vertigo in fact was plainly a chilling experience, and a fairly common human one worth writing about. But I did not like the atmosphere of a fire station yard — too specialized, and for me too personally unpleasant. Then one day I was walking in some part of London and came upon a disused gasometer. Its giant dereliction, its enormous rust, its dreadful vertical ladder relentlessly ascending the side froze me with wonder; that is to say, something more than fear, admiration and fear combined, as with thunderous great music which both threatens and elevates at the same time. And then, again some time later, I was in a park, and watching a group of teenagers fooling about. They were involved in a joke-bet. Who would have the courage to cross that log laid across a small stretch of water? They egged on one of the party, and the most particular egger was a girl. The youth was shamed into beginning his perilous crossing. Three-quarter way across he stopped, swayed, hypnotised by the difficulty of balancing and the sight of that wet, cold water beneath. But the others had already grown tired of the joke and simply strolled off, leaving the poor fellow there teetering at his wit's but not the log's end. Whether he finally fell in or not does not matter — it was the situation of the joke turned sour which abruptly set me thinking and evoked my own memories of vertigo and of the landscape of the derelict gasometre. From that moment the unfortunate young man Clegg began his perilous ascent of the vertical ladder, a long long climb, leaving his aggressive companions below to grow bored and stroll away while he, sweating near the top of the ladder, clung on terribly high in the air in a panic, unable to move further in either direction.

The whole of a story is also about its parts, including its minor parts. You want a small diversion — then introduce what, a tramp, a cat, a fuchsia? You want the colour of an aunt's dress, the kind of trees in a garden? In the selection of such details, I am against the long pen-chewing reverie at the desk, the furious pacing to and fro as carpet-eating shoes stamp and turn to the dread decision: 'Would this be *exactly* right? Or what about *that*?' Put in, I would say, something you came across yesterday.

For that something will be still very much there, bright and palpable, with all its important presence. What it happens to be often makes little difference (unless you intend a symbolic significance – which nowadays will often be too easily spotted, will tread as heavily as those pacing shoes on the study carpet). But how immediate and presenceful the 'something' is does indeed matter. Obviously, not just anything will do. But your recent past will have provided reasonable alternatives. The tramp-cat-fuchsia transposes neatly into the day-before-yesterday's wasp, the aunt's dress is coloured exactly as that girl's on a No 11 last Saturday, the kind of trees are those in the square you walk round most evenings of your otherwise dedendroni-zed life.

Dedendronized! What a word, scrub it out immediately! It is con-fected, it is portentous. Treeless is what it means. Long words for their own sake are a disease: but equally dangerous is their opposite, a sub-slang of baby words popularized by newspapers careful of their laziest readers. Thus we have daily to bear 'see-through', 'sexy', 'know-how' – gormless baby-talk, when there are such reliable old trusties as 'diaphanous', 'erotic' and 'knowledge'. But here we are back with style, and away from the pertinent matter of what to write a story about. Which again proposes a further question often put to the writer: 'What is the personal purpose of your writing? Of your stories? What is your personal impulse in writing them?'

The easy answer is 'to express myself', which covers a multitude of different impulses. Having thought about this a great deal, I can come up with only one true and general answer: to express my wonder at life. One cannot quite say 'love of life', though the feeling is often near to this, for the truth of life is plainly often unloveable. But wonder, amazement, continually astonished interest – these are part of this writer's wish to express not himself but moments of perception at this wonder. I might put it another way — to show the magic or poetry in ordinary things. That often I seem to write about the extraordinary may seem to deny this. But to me it proves the opposite. I have simply made ordinary things sound extraordinary: in fact, conveyed the magic in them. The truth, in fact, is often too bizarre for the page. It has to be watered down to hold water. Look at the small items at the bottom of any newspaper page, and you will understand what I mean. A drunk man in charge of a bulldozer churns up his boss's home. A suburban garden disappears — it has simply caved in above the site of an ancient spring, taking a tea-party, complete with silver teapot and possibly a vicar, along with it. Such affairs must be treated with the utmost diplomacy. They must be toned down, told less than truthfully in the search for a balance of truth. On the other hand, apparently dull stretches of life often have to be toned up: life at the kitchen sink, for a well-known instance, where all is not the colour of dishwater but also the sensuous colour and texture of a wet bar of soap, the iridescence of detergent bubbles, the cymballing of saucepan lids, the applause of the plughole's roar. Or a dull day of rain — it can be laid on, or made occasionally beautiful as the mood dictates: but it can never be left just dull — or if dullness only is intended, then it must be made evocatively dull.

5. When?   And finally — when do you write a story?

There are the lucubrators. There is indeed a very remarkable stillness in a room at night when the town and the family have gone to bed: to those who occasionally meet it on a sleepless night, it is unbelievable. To the regular nightwriter, it is the only possible atmosphere for creation: he feels not only the quiet, but the condition all around of life having paused, of acres of dark nothingness stretching for street after street beyond — he sits in a dry dew of silence where the images in his mind can multiply and come close.

Then there is the very early riser, who has the freshness of dawn and a good night's rest to help him. A sensible expedient indeed, body rested, and the mind enlivened by air comparatively fresh — and it is extraordinary how fresh the air of a petrol-fugged town can be after a

few trafficless hours. But rising so early, if you can bear it, insists on
a reasonably early bedtime, which is often impossible, so that the
superlative importance of a routine is broken. We are not all Trollope,
that fox-hunting dynamo who wrote, between six and eight of a
morning, the equivalent of three modern novels a year, and still had
time and energy to act as postmaster or huntsman throughout the day,
and on top of this take three month's holiday a year.

I belong to none of the above categories, working best in mid-
morning like, I imagine, most people with a nine till five job. There is
a sense of rebirth after a night's sleep, one is at one's daily freshest.
And one must be fresh, for writing is highly exhausting work. In my
time I have done. many a hard day's manual labour; and I can vouch
that three hours' concentrated writing is far more exhausting than
eight hours lifting and carrying heavy iron pipes. In those three hours
of writing the whole body and nerves and, if there is one, soul are
tensed and tautened to the extreme. It is an athletic process, and needs
to be treated so.

Just as it needs to be treated as a regular devotion. The writer who
waits for inspiration and only then rushes to his desk will probably
fail. He is unprofessional. The matter must be otherwise, a day-after-
day regular affair. One must sit down before that blank sheet of paper
and force inspiration to come. Usually, it will. Sometimes the first
few hundred words will prove too forced, and afterwards have to be
replaced; but at least they will have opened the way for the valuable
passages that have followed them. Also, if you are lucky enough to be
a loving calligraphist, then the blank page will not so much terrify as
seduce you. You want to make your mark on it. Typewriters dull me —
noisy and cumbersome and without the pleasures of the visually
creative pen and its guiding fingers.

Naturally, the period of actually writing it all down, those three or
four hours, are not by any means the whole of a writer's day. There is
thinking, dreaming, or formulating exact notes for the following day.
There are proofs of previous work to correct, there are current type-
scripts to re-read with the blue pencil well in hand. There are ordinary
business engagements to do with the sale or syndication of previous

work. There are a hundred other matters to attend to, and on top of this there is the necessity to read and study. No one has ever learned enough. And finally, there is a deal of living to be done, for in that living, far from the printed page, well out of earshot of any literary friends, lies your raw material.

How, then, to make the time for all this? Adding to so already tight a schedule the hours when you are humanly too dull to attend properly?

One of the only rules is to cut down all set social engagements to a very bare minimum. There simply cannot be time to sit through those two-hour executive luncheons, be they working lunches or not. And it is appalling to have to attend a theatre, or have to go to a party, when suddenly you are functioning at your very best. You must be free to function. If you cannot, then take time off spontaneously: time in any case scarcely 'off', because your raw material will be there calling you to work on it. Why did the old-time painter or writer often have long hair? Not for a romantic appearance — that came self-consciously later — but because he could not be bothered with a barber, it wasted time.

I myself carry on this regular routine through the weekends, and through at least the mornings of holidays, taking days off only when I feel physically unfit. Probably the kernel of the matter is that the game is not worth the candle unless you cannot stop yourself writing. Remember, you are always faced with two jobs in one, master and slave. If this collusion is difficult, then you are in trouble indeed. But if the relationship is a happy one, then few ways of life and work can be more rewarding.

In the above general notes, I have kept as far as possible from a textbook atmosphere; and certainly have not covered every facet of writing. Instead, I have gone from point to point, haphazard, as it occurred to me from my own experience, much in the manner of a dialogue, or some sort of solitary seminar. There is today a position in some universities, mostly American, called 'resident writer'. A writer is invited simply to live in the university for a term, carry on with his own work, hold a few seminars, and answer individual questions.

It is not a bad idea. There, in fact, as with a zoo, you have the live thing before your eyes. The remoteness, even deification of Art with a capital A is reduced to human proportions. Here is an ordinary enough figure of a man, who, though gifted in some ways, nevertheless has had to clean his teeth that morning, has a broken shoe-lace, might have had too many martinis the night before: such visible vulnerability brings him to earth, and hopefully his words will be conversational, unposed, removed from the written abstraction of analytical criticism and its jargon of 'characterization' and 'anticlimactic', necessary but nevertheless fleshless contrivances like cyphers spewed from a computer, with which rightly we can soon become impatient. It is somewhat in this spirit that I have tried to put together these notes, as if I were being asked about it, eyeball to eyeball, in a relaxed room.

And now on to the particular, this story called *No Smoking on the Apron*, with a detailed analysis of why I think I wrote it, and how, page by page, it evolved.

NO SMOKING
ON THE APRON

3

No Smoking on the Apron

AIRSOCKS blew out taut as signposts; the apron stretched wide with
wind, a long flat fen of tar and concrete and grass. But Dunko Bates
waited windless with a dozen other passengers at the glass door still
officially closed but through which he would in a minute leave for the
skies, London and home.

Pigskin about. Glossy little luggages in passengers' hands, and parcels
and cartons. These who were spending half a hundred pounds on their
tickets were saving half a whole pound on little bottles of duty-free
alcohol. And in stomachs there wobbled and gurgled unaccustomed
drinks taken to while away the vestibular half-hours of air-travel, and
odd bits of salacious food too—yet all soon to be followed by lunch
at ten-thirty, and so on, Dunko Bates knew it all, the weird palliatives
to this long day of quick communication. And a glucose sweet in the
middle-oh.

Dull, all of it. But he felt now a little excited, or edgy, about this
woman in white who stood to his left and slightly behind him. She
was not pretty, but very attractive. She was smart, and smelled smart:
coloured hair and face, scent, silk, and soft leather, sparked out messages from her. She stood armoured and sure, like an actress, and
dabbed last lipstick on her lips.

Bates smelled her, dismissed her—for what had he, well-married, to
do with painted ladies in aeroplanes?—and watched a fat silver jet-liner
amble about with a blind look, with the blind purpose of a large expectant metal moth looking for somewhere to lay her eggs. Another
plane was whining high, a celestial hoover off-stage. And up swooped
yet another low off the ground, too low it looked—would it ever gain
healthy height?

It would. But there again Dunko knew all about that, the queasy
moment of taking off, the too nonchalant glance down to see that the
trees and roofs had really got small enough, the sudden taste of the

glucose sweet again, the relief heaved. And he remembered his telegram that morning to his wife: *Hope arrive sometime this afternoon.* His conference had ended early, he had been suddenly free of Copenhagen, and had chanced his single luck on the first available plane. And there it was again—he had superstitiously to swallow the thought '*chance my luck* on a plane', just as earlier he had nearly cancelled the phrase '*hope* arrive'. Whatever the statistics said about fewer accidents by plane than by any other form of transport, the whole horrible business still turned him up. Boasting aloud to people 'I'm dead scared of the whole business' did no good either. Every time he went up, until he was right up, he walked out on the apron as with a halter round his neck, fatal, surrendered, ticketed, docketed and doomed. The other passengers were no help—they easily assumed the appearance of in- sentient cattle herded witless to their fate. And the fixed knowing smiles of the hostess and steward were false as a nurse's death-cheer.

The woman in white did not seem so troubled. She was still working away with the lipstick, sucking her lips in, legs braced firmly back on high heels. He went once more over his preparations, passport, ticket, briefcase, bag, flight docket—and then remembered his fountain pen. It always leaked under height-pressure. He looked at the floor. No carpet. A drop of ink wouldn't harm?

He took the pen out and uncapped it. But just as he pressed the lever, the door to the field was swung open, a great gust of Baltic air blew in, the spitting ink was caught in mid-drop and blown sideways to splatter a rich blue tatoo all over that woman's white dress.

'Aaah,' she gasped.

Her fine shoulders square: 'You—you great—clumsy—idiot,' she gasped. 'You idiotic *fool*.'

At the same time she raised her hand to mark her point, jabbing him with it as she repeated, 'You'll pay, pay, *pay* for this. . . .'

And she repeated it and it was the hand that held the lipstick that jabbed him, all over his lapels, his shirt, and as high as his collar as her face reached up close to his. 'Aaah,' she sighed, at last receding, while he stammered apologies.

Then: 'I say,' he said, 'I mean, really,' as he looked down at his shirt and suit now daubed with red.

So there they stood, panting for breath and words, the two of them red, white and blue as a drunkard's eye.

But just then the door was officially opened, an official chanted once again the flight number and beckoned them out to the apron, and there they had to go.

As they walked out, quickly—for each passenger must hurry, though without seeming to, without running, to be first for the best place in the plane—the woman snapped at him:

'What's your name and address?'

Grimly he swung his briefcase and bag into one hand, fumbled in his waistcoat and gave her a card. Like a dueller, she whipped into her bag and gave him hers.

By that time they had reached the stairway into the plane. Tow-haired men made of pork and beer stood underneath tending long pipes fixed into the aircraft's belly: like flaxen farmers, they seemed to be mechanically milking this fine fat silver aphis. As he stepped aside to let the woman walk up the stairs first, Dunko noted with pleasure the goose-pimpling of rivets that studded the machine's silver body all over, so very many, so secure.

There were few passengers. Dunko and the woman each had a double seat to their separate selves.

She sat just behind the starboard wing, he a little further back to port. Ordinarily now Dunko would have glanced up at the little lighted words telling him not to smoke and to get ready for the crash by fastening his seat-belt. Followed by the reassurance of the captain's name written up in solid letters, a trick that really worked, because, thus named, this man must bear all responsibility for any mishandling. And he would have looked out along the wing to make sure nothing was falling off. And he would have caught sight of the airport building, suddenly now a dull contemptible place full of landlubbers eating and drinking. But today all these routines—and the quick look through the pamphlets and sickness bag in the web pocket in front—all were purged by new anxieties. For of course the woman was quite right to flare at him so. Yes, yes, quite right—though it had been an accident.

Nevertheless . . . what would such a dress cost? Would he have to buy her another? Where? Paris? He tried desperately to subdue his sense of fair play and find a way out. But there was none evident.

Then he remembered something else. There was this lipstick all over him . . . and what kind of a reception might he thus receive from his dearly loved at home? On the threshold, between twin tubbed bay-trees in the light of an electrified carriage lamp, at the primrose door? Slashed with rouge?

He would never be able to blame his wife for what she might think. So there he sat, not blaming two women; and the plane slightly shuddered as it slid smoothly off towards the runway.

The uneasy thought of a hundred pounds for a dress had to be put aside in consideration of a greater loss, that of his wife. Yet wives and husbands, assumably in each other's confidence, should surely be able to discuss so absurd a story, and to laugh about it? But was there not a too privately amused twist to his wife's lips as he stammered through the whole ridiculous rigmarole, and a certain half-light of fear in her eyes afterwards, when hollowly they had laughed together about the whole thing? And in any case, surely the episode was a trifle *too* ridiculous to be quite believed? Damn life, he thought, that is made up so much of these trip-rope absurdities, rather than seriously heroic traps. Why couldn't he, just for once, be permitted to save someone from drowning? Where were the runaway horses at whose heads to throw himself? Life the bloody banana-skin, he thought.

The captain was turning the plane around, and as at other times Dunko might have looked up at the little red emergency-door notices, he now went through all possible routes from this far more frightening problem. It was a Sunday, so he could not buy a new shirt. Wait—what about the East End, Petticoat Lane? No, shut by the afternoon. Bitterly he cursed the drip-dry age that sent him abroad with only one shirt and a footling plastic hanger. Then—could he perhaps bribe a shirt from someone? He foresaw the affronted surprise at such effrontery, the long explanations. It made him tired to think of it. Impossible. Well then, a hotel showcase? But on a Sunday afternoon no one would have the key, and there would surely be some Act forbidding a Sunday sale. Moreover, there would be no shirts in the cases of any hotels *he* chose, there would be only ties, and socks, and diamonds; everything but shirts. To think, ten years ago, of all the bachelor friends he could easily have telephoned! Now not one left, all married up. In any case, even if a sabbatical London in some fantastic fashion were made to yield up a shirt, it would be too much to ask a suit of it: and his, pale grey, was indelibly daubed with red.

Then, as at last he surrendered to his predicament, a dark thought came to him. He did not admit it; but nevertheless it propelled him, he rose up, crossed the carpeted gangway, and sat down beside that woman in white.

'Now we're more settled,' said Dunko, 'I'd like to say how very sorry I am about your dress. I really am. It was,' he said, 'a most unfortunate incident, accident.'

It was only good manners, he repeated to himself—still draping his unadmitted intention with this excuse of apologizing to a lady. Yet what was he doing with his face—flashing his eyes, glittering his teeth, revving up a kind of charm-engine inside him?

'We're on fire,' she said.

Who? Him?

'There!' she gasped, grabbing his arm and pointing out along the wing. A tongue of flame was spitting from behind one of the engines.

His heart jumped. He never liked the look of that. But he had seen it often before, and now laughed reassurance at the woman. 'Not to worry,' he said, 'it's only—' but he never quite knew what it was—'overflow petrol burning off,' he guessed.

She smiled now. 'I'm sorry,' she said, 'silly of me.'

'No, it's I who am sorry. And silly. Won't you have a drink?'

'Well, I don't—'

'Good,' he said, and rang the steward's bell.

By the time they had each drunk a double *snaps*—after her protestations against such early spirits, and his overruling that lunch would be served unearthly, ha ha literally unearthly, soon, and he was ringing the bell for more—they had ceased to discuss the incident of the ink and were talking enjoyably of other things.

The plane was high in the skies. They had been too occupied to notice much the differing roars and whines of the engine: only once, at the vital moment of leaving the ground, Dunko had halted in mid-sentence, observing a ritual silence, and a second later had glanced very casually through the porthole to make sure they had achieved a proper height. And the woman, ignorant of the meaning of this moment, more ready to fear changes of noise and lurchings, had asked him if he was all right?

'Quite,' he said.

She had laughed: 'For a moment I thought you were going to be sick.'

So it was as apparent as that? 'Never sick,' he said, 'the sick bags are too valuable. I'm making a little collection of them. My favourites are the Swedish FOR SYK, and the remarkably suggestive Portuguese— PARA ENJOO.'

'Suggestive?'

'Sort of enjoyment and goo, with a parachute thrown in for good measure. Have a nice time while you're at it.'

Luckily, she leered at this. But what was he up to, getting on to goo when he had meant to be at his most charming? Charming—for what had passed through Dunko's mind earlier was to be hanged for a sheep as well as a lamb. Thus, if his loved one at home was going to accuse him of sexual infidelity, then sexually infidel he might as well be. It was the injustice of it all that impelled him. He had managed to conceive and to fortify a picture of his wife's scowling face, quite unjustly. Well—if Sheila wanted to take *that* sort of attitude, if she refused outright even to try to understand his position—then at least he would get his money's worth, he would go ahead and flirt fit to bust with this woman in white.

'I travel a lot,' he said, 'on business.'

'What are you in?'

'Shrimps—that is, frozen shellfish.'

'Mm! Num.'

'You like them? Then I must certainly send you some—remember, I've got your card, Miss—' he looked at it, 'oh, *Mrs* Cabot.'

'Just a wife.'

'Just?'

'A wife with ten days in Denmark behind her. An uneventful ten days,' she murmured, frowning, and smiling to herself.

'Why uneventful?'

He looked out at the wing flapping rubbery, and again applauded the amount of rivets, the silver cleanliness—and looked back at her, pleased with her strong pleasant face, firm-chinned and softened by dark blue eyes brightened by black lashes. She wore a very white powder, under a very black fringe. And the red lipstick, the whiteness of face and dress, and the blue eyes and come to that the spattering his own blue ink gave her something of the look of a large child in party dress—white, red and blue: or one of those old-style Gallic prostitutes who wore the tricolore ribbon in black hair above their white shifts, and a tricolore garter on black stockings. It was, he supposed, the dark fringe that emphasized these effects. But surely she could not be English?

'Is England your home now?' he asked.

'Why uneventful?' she said, still considering his question. 'Why, I've never been able to get over that adolescent expectation that something should *happen* on a trip abroad, You know?'

'I think I do,' he murmured. Abroad. She spoke English perfectly.

'Oh yes I'm English,' she added—and this was wonderful, how their thoughts were meeting!—'always lived there. Though I've a Belgian mother.'

So it took no more than a Belgian mother to do all this? He marvelled. And thrilled.

'But this time nothing, nothing, nothing happened,' she said, and shot him a dark amused glint from her blue-black inky eyes.

He returned her a knowing look, the plane thrummed, the sun now shone in holiday-hot above a far-reaching cotton sea of cloud, and lunch was served.

A while later, after they had fiddled with a dwarf's set of small square dishes and pixie pepperpots, he presented her with his foil-wrapped triangle of processed cheese. She accepted. He assured her he had eaten enough, and surely the triangle should not be left to the profit of the air company? It was all rather exciting, intimate—sharing food, like tried lovers eating from the same plate.

'I don't like flying,' he said over a goblin's tumbler of brandy, 'but I shall never cease to marvel at our being suspended in air in such a heavy intricate machine full of carpets and lavatories. If you could put your finger out through the window, it would be blasted off by frost alone. Yet here we sit snuggly and warm. Control of the skies! You've got to hand it to man.'

Snuggly was good. They two together snuggly.

'Ah,' she said, 'if only man would learn to control himself as well.'

They two together deeply philosophic! But having sighed profoundly, he turned her last remark. Deftly.

'It's sometimes too difficult for him,' he murmured looking straight into her eyes: which, after a lost second, she lowered modestly.

'We're approaching a small patch of bad weather,' said the captain's disembodied voice, 'it will be more comfortable if everyone would please fasten their seatbelts.'

Instant hush. Then a rise of chatter as everybody flinched or boasted. Let's hope man controls himself now, Dunko thought, as he smiled reassuringly at Mrs Cabot, who had gone a shade whiter than usual. 'Nothing untoward,' he told her, with his big lazy smile. Alone, he would have felt apprehensive. But now great protective muscles bunched all over him, he felt athletically capable of dealing with any terror, now that this more frightened person was by his side.

'How on earth does he know?' she asked, looking out at the clear blue sky and the cloud below.

'Wireless telegraphy,' he said casually.

Why not 'radio'? But then radio was a brittle word, it sounded too much like a modern air-crash headlined by efficient newspapers. Whereas the other suggested old leather and vulcanite contraptions, crystal sets that battled like good camping equipment, bending with the elements, elastic, true.

Then the windows all turned black as night, the plane took a terrible plunge, banged down on a floor of something, shook to burst, and then raced its engines as if climbing a hill.

She was digging her fingers into his wrist. Big-muscled still, but the blood drained from his gills, he put his other hand over hers, hairy and comforting. When the next lurch came, she buried her face between his lapel and armpit: powder, and more rouge, sunk into his suit.

He felt genuinely tender then towards her, and braver in himself. As a virtue of sin is to provoke virtue in others, so fear in others has made many a coward a brave man—this infection of opposites brought the blood back to Dunko's cheeks and he was able to mutter warmly, without a tremor:

'Not to worry. All quite usual. A bit of an electric storm.'

The plane took a terrible lurch to one side, then rose, racing again, then dropped flat as a runaway lift—everyone rose in their seats, a briefcase flew through the air, cups clattered horribly, blackness flew by the portholes, and the pilot began zooming this way and that like a hook-mad barracuda weaving fast through ink-dark deep water.

'Quite usual,' Dunko said, and stroked her hair.

They reared and plunged on. A woman was quietly sobbing some-where, a man was ringing the bell over-jovially for a brandy 'to top up', the hostess was flitting to and fro along the carpeted gangway with a set toothpaste smile plastered where her mouth should have been. Dunko glanced at her eyes for signs of fear, but, as always, they bore no expression at all.

There was something appalling about the electric lights still blazing all over what now felt a very small cigar-shaped roomlet, a miniature tube-train run wild in a tunnel. Yet how much worse if all these lights had gone out! Dunko massaged his Mrs Cabot and glanced efficiently up at the red-marked emergency exit opposite the next seat along—but how in the devil to open it? Push what? And how to get round in front of the two people sitting there? What did one do—stiffen the upper lip and queue?

'There!' he said, as they zoomed out into pure blue daylight.

'Oh God,' she said, straightening herself up and withdrawing her hand quite sharply.

She was offended with him for having been there to witness her lack of control. But this passed, the stronger fact of bodily contact, the intimacy of aeroplanes, the escapade of voyage—for in its condensed way, a plane-trip had the liberalizing effect on the romantic strings of a sea-voyage—these brought them closer together, so that soon their knees were touching and he was murmuring without shame such sweet everythings as 'your lapis lazul eyes'. Flirting had given way to something far fleshier; and Dunko had quite forgotten his earlier reservations, as success took its exhilarating toll.

'I'm so glad we caught fire,' he chuckled.

'What? We *didn't!*'

'I mean, when we began, remember? Along the wing? Otherwise you'd still have been at me over your dress, confess!'

She laughed. 'Oh that,' she said, ink-blue eyes lowered on to ink-stains.

'Where did you get it?' he asked. 'It looks so marvellous!'

Flattered, and proud of her own clever buy, she said: 'A little place round the corner—two pounds seventeen and six!'

'Good heavens!' he said, really pleased for her. An hour earlier he would have felt relief: but now such a matter, the debt or no of a hundred pounds, was lost in the bloodrush. And the air dashed by as their great silver cigar crossed high above more and more sea rippling tiny below, far-below skin wrinkled on a grey old hand, with lost ships like scattered moles—to England, Home and London Airport.

But when she went to wash her hands, he was left for a moment with thoughts of his true predicament, and of his wife; and his stomach felt guiltily empty. Then she was back, there and lovely in the flesh, and he felt hot and handsome as before. But the guilty memory of Sheila dovetailing into Mrs Cabot made him notice that they were both of the same colouring, two editions as it were of the same thing, and he felt both more betraying and somehow faithful at the same time.

By the time the captain was telling them they were passing over the English coast and on time, Dunko and Mrs Cabot knew a superficial lot about each other, where they lived and what they liked. She did not comment on her husband, she simply kept off the subject. So did he.

But she lived in Cumberland, and had to spend the night in London. . . .

They peered down at the very green plan of London beneath—it seemed to be a clean and fresh-built garden city—and then the no-smoking sign lit up, the seat-belts went on, the runway came up to meet them. As always, Dunko averted his eyes from this. And this time he used the occasion to stare long and fixedly into hers. Then—bumpety-bump went the wonderful rubber wheels, they whizzed smooth along, and the engines at last reversed. It was the moment of safety. 'Ah,' he said, with a look of pleasure. She took this to mean relief at a journey, their journey together, ended—and such a small sign of his interest ending helped to accelerate in her an idle thought, a wish, an idea. The idea became, vaguely, a decision.

Landings, arrivals . . . no night richness of a city of red and yellow jewels beneath, no mystery of blue lamps studding like magic marsh-gas the barren flat dark field—no, here was simply London air in day-light, stale inland air after the salt breezes of Denmark. In the aircraft they shuffled up among coats and hangers in the thick silence left by the engine's last pop. They endured the frank-eyed good-byes of the hostess and steward, so intendedly personal as to end up precisely in-human; stepped down the stairs marvelling again at the size of the now so quiet big beast that had carried them so far—it was neither sweating, nor puffing—and walked together among other passengers clutching their duty-free packages towards the big solid brick airport building. Isolated on the broad field, the trailing little group wound like a lonely funeral party escaping from its own coffin.

'Within walking distance!' he found himself saying. 'Lucky we didn't have to get one of those awful tarmac buses. They're awful, those awful buses, after you've come so far so quick.'

She touched his arm tenderly and smiled her strong smile.

'Are you taking the other bus, up to the terminal?' she asked.

He nodded, as she continued: 'My hotel's just by the terminal. I'll make a bargain; if you taxi me there, I'll give you a drink. Fair?' she proposed brightly, as with good clean fun.

As she said this, he saw across her shoulder a big notice: NO SMOKING ON THE APRON.

'Fair?' he laughed. 'It's dyed-in-the-wool blonde. Let's wash it in beer!'

Phew! And with that notice rumbling at him! And what if the apron smokes on *you,* Dunko-boy?

And in the arrival lounge, and up against the quiet grey-eyed passport officer in his misleading tweeds, and with the sharply polite customs men in their peaked caps, he again saw the writing on the wall: Dunko Go Home.

She had put more of that scent on. She felt to him, on this firm dull unmoving earth, more attractive than ever—and she moved so well, that had been the first thing he had noticed back at the other airport.

It was still early in the day. There was the whole afternoon. The two usual sensations of the arrived fought inside him—that he must hurry, hurry home now by this slow bus-and-taxi business after the wind-whistling aircraft: and the opposite, that here was terra firma upon which you could spread yourself, stroll across to buy a paper, with all time hanging about slow as fog after the fleet minutes of aluminium flight. Along with these immediate sensations, his real responsible and equally real delinquent sides fought for place. After all—it was only for a drink? And time did not press?

So he stood at the terminal, fiddling. Fiddling in his mind: and his pockets too. Should one throw what ticket, what label away? Aeroplanes left one's pockets full of paper. He stood fiddling, and meanwhile two taxis had drawn up. Not asking, the porter put both their luggages into the first taxi, and she said: 'Gaylor's Hotel, off the Cromwell Road there,' so that who could blame him for not expostulating, rearranging, good-byeing—and with the queue behind for other taxis? Who? He well knew who.

But now also the body came to help these mental worries, it said he wanted a drink and—as this very thought rose to mind, conscious and alert, Dunko squeezed her knee in the cab jerking and buzzing not at all slowly towards Gaylor's.

He went to choose a table for them in the lounge while she signed the register. But she interrupted, looked round the big room with a brr sound and a shiver, and bade him come up to her room, for she must in any case unpack a few dresses immediately. 'I *have* others, in reserve,' she smiled.

Up in her room, as she walked about active and decided, placing her handbag there and parcels here, and ordering the drinks which came almost immediately, Dunko did not know whether to stand or to sit and if to sit, to sit on what. So he went to the mirror, and combed his hair with his fingers.

'Drink!' she said, handing him a glass. 'There's more on the tray—I'll only be two ticks in the bathroom, get this blotter of yours off my back.'

But she came back not in another dress but a peignoir.

They drank. Then, having so far fixed the material scene, she advanced no further. Swept off his feet by so sudden and apparently brazen a succession of events—taxi, lift, shut door, drinks, peignoir—he found himself expected to put his best foot forward.

Daylight came grey through the window, but golden whisky made nightlight inside him. And all around was the excitation of unfamiliar feminine scents and objects—she had already emptied a leather case of cosmetics and bottles out on to the dressing-table. All this made for terrible silences. Once they both started talking together; and broke with laughter at this. The laughter was too loud, hysterical, and only emphasized the next patch of silence.

He looked at her, and felt suddenly sad. It seemed both exciting and pathetic. Rooms, rooms, men and women everywhere, all doing the same kind of thing. Each unique, each the same.

'Blast,' he gasped, and took her in his arms and kissed her for a long dark time. 'No,' she groaned, 'no,' and drew him closer. The peignoir slid apart and they lay back on the bed and made love, while occasionally voices passed muffled in the corridor outside and a sound of plates washing echoed up from the kitchens far below the window, and the sun far above in the sky wheeled lower and lower until just before its landing it shone low through the window and turned the wallpaper to dying, dead gold.

He got up and opened his own flask of duty-free whisky and poured two drinks. They sat on the edge of the bed and drank, talking a little too brightly, laughing, but kissing no more. They both felt sad, and the room seemed strangely empty.

A little later, he said good-bye. They still had each other's cards, and said so in mutual consolation, but the duel was plainly over.

He was home.

She ran to him, all brightness like a big little dog, and hugged and kissed him, kissed and kissed, snuggling and snuffling, stroking his chest with her soft cheek.

'Oh darling, darling, darling!'

And then: 'Oh *darling* what a *filthy* mess I've made of you . . . your shirt . . . your *suit* . . . oh Dunk what a *beast* I am. . . .'

4

How the Story was Written

The story was written in the autumn of 1961. For some years previously I had been commissioned to write occasional essays on places abroad, and this had meant a lot of flying. In fact, I knew well the atmosphere of airplanes, airports and air travellers. Though decried by so many as neutral and lifeless, these seemed to me to have a strong atmosphere, both in their material landscape and the emotions provoked inside the human cargo; I found myself wanting to write it all down.

But I did not want to approach it in a too technical manner, to discover secrets of the organization of airports or of the mechanisms of planes, the lives of pilots and hostesses. I preferred to rely on my own experience as an ordinarily ignorant customer canalized through and into the air.

Also, from a dramatic point of view, I did not want to write violently of anything like a crash, or someone going mad, or of heart attacks or gunning. I wanted the experience to be ordinary. But no kind of plot or personal situation occurred to me to set the thing in motion. So it was laid to rest, ticking over very quietly in the back of my mind.

At the same time, or at various times through the years, I had reflected on another matter — the often awkward circumstances of a chance love affair between a man and woman. Apart from the stock situations of a party or a holiday, it seemed unlikely to occur at a time convenient to both of them. I well remember from my youth how often, when chance had introduced me to a girl and we had hit it off, I had been too broke that day to prolong the meeting, or she had some pressing appointment. Perhaps the frustration and regret of these occasions make them memorable; perhaps they are equated by other more successful meetings. Nevertheless, they did occur. And they left me with the complementary belief that the man who goes pounding up to the bright lights on Friday nights with his pay packet in his pocket is really equally uncertain of finding his nymph errant: he may easily meet a girl, but not any kind of *the* girl. Love and liking are not so orderly as this. Chance meetings occur at the chanciest times.

So that the general thought, or theme if you like, was ticking over too. And then came the day when I happened to be cleaning out a fountain pen. The ink was pressed out, I was standing by a door to the garden, I was wearing white trousers, a sudden summer breeze blew up, a blob of ink flew down dangerously near those laundered white legs.

As instantly, a plot flew into position. What perils lie in a pen, clicked the computing mind! And where does one empty a pen? At airports. And what valuable material would be spoiled by the flying ink blob? A white dress flew into being, complete with a woman inside it, and somehow associatively, perhaps because of the blueness of the ink, a red and white face with ink-blue eyes. The associations were gathering, the episode occurred at the door of an airport lounge where the wind from the field blew in, and the owner of the ink blob became, in complement to a woman, a man. A shadowy me stepped inside the shadowy man, who is never described in detail, so that a shadowy reader can as easily step inside him too. The scene was set.

And what was to happen? The whole question of chance meetings arose; something, I did not know what, would happen to these two. But first, an obvious altercation about the ink stain on her dress, and most certainly, from a background point of view, a full exposition of the ordinary fears and bravados of two human beings offering their soft bodies to the steel of a machine, the vast drop of the skies.

At that point, I would have gone to my desk and jotted down a note or two condensing the above. If I do not do this, the whole matter is too easily forgotten altogether. But it is also important for me that the notes are no more than a telegraphic message. Notes can be dangerous. If they are written out in full, they can too easily also fulfil the function of writing the idea out of oneself.

It is the same with journals; if you write into them what you are writing about, then you have already written it, and the first valuable impulse to get it down on paper, to express it, is gone. (A similar

danger is talking about what you should be writing about: many a
writer talks himself out of himself, and thereafter the pages lie fallow.
How the French, who are adept at this, manage, this reticent norther-
ner cannot know. Mysteriously, they do. Personally, I cannot. I never
talk about my current work, even to my wife. The need to express
would simply be gone, or at best dangerously diluted.)

Now there had to be a further period of waiting, until the desk was
cleared of whatever work was going on when this first note was taken.
Occasionally, though, the note would be picked up, and the day-
dream continued. Such a short and telegraphic note usually has a
magical capacity for bringing to mind again its whole more complicated picture: as with the simple time and place of an engagement
noted once in a diary, it recalls the whole scene and mood of a hitherto
unremembered day.

During such fairly idle re-consideration of the note, more facts
would have been jotted down: probably a short list of visual aspects
of an airfield — the rivets in the silver wings, the big-moth look of
planes blundering about. The 'celestial hoover' sounds of high-circling
aircraft. Also a memory of recent bumpy flights — one from Norway,
in an electric storm, one from Lisbon in blue calm. Unfortunately in
this case, while as you see both manuscript and typescript of the story
are preserved, the notes were destroyed. But I know pretty well what
they would have been like.

What, however, is important is that I relied on memory for the airfield and airplane setting. I did not go to an airport and take new
notes. They would have swamped themselves. Memory fulfils a useful
function in cancelling away what may be superfluous. When, for instance, I write an essay on a foreign city, I never write it either on
the spot or immediately on return home. It can ride, until such time
as it can be reviewed in the cool perspective of that city seen from
home, and as a contrast to home, and thus from any reader's point of
view; what is most important from this double vantage point — the
notes taken there, the desk at home — will stand out naturally. Unimportant details, over-exciting when you are abroad, will go. Memory
provides a natural sieve.

Eventually the moment comes when the desk is clear for the writing of the story. The afternoon or evening before, I take out whatever notes have been made and review them. They will not be very many: usually no more than, say, a dozen items. Possibly a query against a potential plot idea; in this case, there was none that I remember.

What the notes now provided were attitudes to take: that the story should be told largely from the mind and experience of a male traveller (the shadow of myself); that some trouble should follow the fountain pen incident; that the flight should at some point be bumpy; that the chance meeting of the man and the woman should be in some way developed and resolved — I did not know how. Let them, I thought, or hoped, see to that themselves.

One good narrative ploy was already inbuilt: the naturally intriguing setting of someone beginning a journey. Thus, in the first paragraph, adventure is implied. This man is going somewhere, so something will happen. As simple as that. It is an inevitable assumption in the reader's mind, a gift to the writer, and, for me, a convenient sop to the dramatist *manqué*. Remember, I *could* have taken the beginning further back, with the male character, say, at a meeting with business associates against the landscape of a foreign city. But I decided against this. Decided to plunge straight into the drama of an airport, a journey. It is, of course in any case a good rule to cut what is superfluous to the main story; apart from diversions, usually when the story is well under way, which might be necessary to slow down too fast a pace, pace developed into speed.

Now the scene had to be seen in detail. The man's name, for instance? I usually prefer one-syllable names. They seem less parochial, less full of a borrowed personality; one syllable cyphers making it easier for the reader to step inside the character.

Often I do not bother about a Christian name; a surname alone seems to give a more solid presence to the person portrayed. You are only formally introduced — and this implies there is more to be found out. But in this particular case I wanted to be intimate from the start, make the man convivial and easy to meet, and also, by choosing a nickname-Christian-name, to infer from the beginning some of the jovial bravado with which many a citizen faces a flight. I had a friend called Duncan: only that week I had heard him spoken to, facetiously, as Dunko. It sounded odd at the time. It stuck. So he was put down as air-traveller, and his one-syllable surname was added probably for euphonious reasons, a 'tes' sound after the ease of 'unko'.

Which airport? Earlier that year, flying from Sweden to Hamburg, I had come down for an hour or so at Copenhagen. For one forgotten reason or other, it photographed well in memory. Perhaps this was because it was a transit visit, a waiting one with leisure to look around. Although I do remember being impressed that the ordinary sensation of flatness on an airfield was enhanced by the feeling of the flatness of the whole of Denmark and its surrounding seas, Denmark whose one distant eminence, far away from Copenhagen, is only five hundred feet high yet called by the flat Danes the Sky Mountain.

So Copenhagen it was, and the story was begun. But I have forgotten one matter – the title. In this case I had the title in mind from the very beginning: it was a phrase posted up at London Airport which I found both striking and funny (in the loose sense that anything to do with kippers, sausages, aprons is in England traditionally a sign for broad humour) and it also had a brooding sense of guilt about it. This matched the two brooding senses of danger, of air flight itself and of the conflict of the protagonists, which should threaten throughout the story.

Having a readymade title is a help, though by no means necessary. It satisfies the instinct of the child everyone still is to put something at the head of the blank page, and decorate it mentally with red ink. It is a first step, starts you off, kills off the emptiness of the page. But if none immediately and naturally occurs, titles should be thought of last, when you know what the story is really about. And they should state what the story is about, not simply enjoy themselves in their artful phrasing. People refer to a book not by the title, if it is far from the subject, but by the subject itself: 'His book about the . . . .' Once I wrote a novel about a man falling in love with a woman seen at a window. I called it *The Loving Eye*. In every translation in widely different countries it was called *The Woman at the Window*. Similarly, a novel about jealousy, which I called *The Body,* was translated, simply and rightly, as *Jealousy.* So, if we want readers to pass on the great news from mouth to mouth, it is wise to cut down here on the aesthetics. A title is not part of the work, its only and great importance is that of a poster, a reference.

I may as well confess at this point, for it will affect most of the detail of this story, that such decisions as the man's name, the choice of airport, the manner of beginning did not involve any great pen-chewing and anxious thought. These processes are quick. A few alternatives may come to mind, flicking past in as few seconds, but the right one is chosen without further hesitation. Things seem to slide into place. Instinct, or the amalgam of all you have so far learned of life, I believe to be more reliable than long and conscious analysis. Too much striving too easily ends in sterility. By this, I do not intend that it is all easy: for you are necessarily tensed up and hard at it to produce the climate for instinct to work at its best.

In any case, the hardest work − for me, at least − comes with the final shaping of the prose, a difficult mixture of instinct and conscious criticism. I envy those writers whose manuscripts I have seen without a single correction. They are few. They were − thinking at random − dictated by necessity: one written in the Kaiser War trenches, when every scrap of paper was at a premium; the other by an authority on Chinese aesthetics who naturally adopted the Chinese technique of long, long concentration and composition in the mind, before the long-poised brush is allowed to paint down an already well-formed result. But most writers chip away like sculptors.

Back to the text − a man is about to leave for the skies. There is a sense of trouble unstated, implicit. Originally, the manuscript interpolated a Danish word-sign seen on the door. I cut it. Its very italics and its alien look held up the flow − in any case, a word about the door being officially still closed was more important. And then straight on, in paragraph two, to the phrase: 'Pigskin about'. This was intentionally dramatic. As if pieces of luggage were on the watch, like detectives. Which led naturally to a line or two describing the atmosphere of travellers on the wait, to make the reader feel himself there, and the final word 'middle-oh' with the 'oh' part to bring us back chattily into the inside of Dunko Bates' mind.

Enter the woman, immediately. She is not described in detail, but definitively as a presence, the particular presence of many women found among the daily air-route passengers (not the carnival holiday haul) whose feminity stands out strong and erotic against the mechanical and mostly male background, in much the same way as a female presence is enhanced in business offices by a background of filing cabinets, documents and desks.

Then quickly the question of Bates dismissing her — what had he to do with painted ladies in aeroplanes? — suggesting, of course, the opposite, that there is going to be plenty between these two.

The scene and the action thus set, there is time to suspend it and begin painting in a background. Bates himself need not be described, but it is as well to say why he is there at all, to stand him on a plinth of credibility. And this is followed by a definite statement of the basic fears of most travellers faced with the skies. The woman, though, is not at all scared: she has the apparently contained carapace of all dolled up women, proof against anything or anyone.

Now the episode of the fountain pen and the flying ink. I remember being a little worried about a man dropping a mess of ink on a public floor — but persisted, thinking it excusable in the heat of the travelling moment, with no carpet, with the heel of a shoe to erase it like a lit cigarette stub. (I see in the manuscript that excuses like 'rough concrete', 'hard stuff' were finally cut out.)

The woman's lipstick was unpremeditated. It was there in her hand to emphasise her smartness, her chic made-upness . . . and then she very naturally began to stab at Dunko with it. And naturally it could be red. A bit of luck, this, which finally took a large place in the whole story. It also served as part of a kind of classic symbol, in the way an architectural façade can employ classical motifs for stability and secure acceptance — here the red, white and blue of the national flag.

The exchange of cards, simulating duellers, was also unpremeditated. It came simply from studying in the mind's eye what such figures, walking over the tarmac, would do. Faintly ridiculous, too — for I wanted to underline a kind of absurd theatricality in the situation. The exchange was also helpful in reminding us that indeed a duel between the two was begun: and suggesting that it must continue, perhaps in the air, and finally end — how?

Most of this time — though only two pages — there has been movement, physical forward movement, in itself a material help to narrative.

Back again now into the man's mind (and the reader's) as he approaches near the looming reality of the aircraft itself. This is a moment always larger than life. It was necessary to dwell on it. Yet natural fears must be compensated for by an equally natural wish for security — false? — and this is found in the rivets, in the comfort of settling down in comfortable seats. A brief recall of the sensations and little terrors of leaving the ground; but quickly a reminder that his present uncertainty of the encounter with this woman overcame even these strong air-frights: money fears, now, and fears of his wife's reception of his lipstick-stained self.

The plane leaves the ground — and once again the narrative is left in slight suspense as Dunko tries mentally to excuse himself in his wife's eyes, these thoughts finally propelling him towards the woman. During this, an edginess of danger has again been inferred — his desire for heroism in the face of some perilous situation — and there is also a detailed exposition of the difficulties of buying a new shirt on a Sunday, a down-to-earth practical detail to reinforce the credibility of what might hitherto have seemed simply too bizarre an incident.

All such touches were not premeditated, but occurred during the time it takes physically to write down the factual sentences. The writer's mind is occupied by two very different matters at the same time, the formation of prose, and the precise detail of the picture of the moment and the immediate future and the movements of these two figures pre-eminent in the no longer simply silver but highly coloured screen of the mind.

Perhaps there is a pause for thought. With me, not always much. I pause more over detailed descriptions rather than over what happens next: but the writer has to look closely for detail, order the film-cutter to slow-down on a close-up. Thus, I had to inspect that Sunday shirt-shop situation closely and consciously. It was not familiar to me. I had to stop and work out what was and what was not possible on an English Sunday. A detail, but very necessary to get right, so that the fiction-writer's invaluable glass baby, that old 'suspension of disbelief', should be in no danger of fragmentation.

Now Dunko (we have long lost the Bates, he is intimate and should be part of us) moves over to the woman, not by some false coincidence of a dropped handkerchief, but intentionally, with an intentional excuse to himself. Though he knows his real intentions are otherwise.

It would, I thought, be dull here to go through any polite interchange without first some exhibition of drive to personalize the woman: and it happened that this was also the moment when that fearful-looking jet of fire from the engines can occur. It is always dramatic in dialogue for a speaker not to answer the other but interrupt with his or her own thoughts: here there was a double chance of slight drama, with the cry of fire and at the same time a deflection of Dunko's overweening charm.

And there follows an introduction to what is one of the themes of the story — the sublimation of personal fear in the duty to prevent fear in others.

The aircraft gains height and the two travellers gain acquaintance-ship. But what should they talk about? In went a fact from my own experience — I happen to have made a casual collection of sick-bags: it seemed a suitably wry subject to pepper the dangerously saccharine moments of man-woman get-together. It also showed Dunko as an awkward suitor, no trained Lothario; and it is followed by his trumped up excuse to himself for the infidelity of flirtation. Thus he is stated as a man of ordinary human weaknesses. In the slight way of flirtation he deceives his wife and himself at the same time.

By now more facts are needed about the background of these two people. In a novel, it is natural to discover this in some detail. In a short story, it should be cut down to a minimum. We have already, very much in passing, learned of Dunko's smartish middle-class house with its primrose door and electrified carriage lamp; now we find that his business is in shrimps (shrimps bracket with kippers as being faintly laughable: but the titter is quickly suppressed into 'frozen shell-fish', a reasonable import from fishy Scandinavia). In return, the lady now gets a name, a married state, a more detailed appearance, empha-sizing again that effect of red, white and blue.

I think that this red, white and blue emphasis was simply dictated by the physical facts of a white dress, blue ink and red lipstick. And, as I have said, repeated as a kind of minor architectural device to help solidify the story. But there is much that goes on in a writer's subcon-cious of which he is ignorant. Did I, I wonder now, have some deep impulse to make two provident, possibly conservative middle-class protagonists let down the Flag? Such unconscious wishes are very possible, though the critic in depth is often tempted to delve too deeply for them, fall in love with whatever treasure he finds, and ex-aggerate his guess-work into established fact.

Since this is guess-work it cannot matter much: although it is in fact concerned with subconscious impulses which are perhaps the most intriguing mystery of all writing, the writing within, the unanalysable, a perpetual mystery never to be solved. I have been astonished to find suspicious cases of it in re-reading my own writings — for instance in a book *Hans Feet in Love,* which turns out to be full of teeth and dogs with teeth which I never consciously intended. Unknown to me, did I deeply want to bite the central character into more determined action, wake him up? Or did I want him to be eaten up? I shall never know. Similarly, with an earlier novel, long after it was written I found that as many as four of the five central characters had, at one time or another, blood on their faces. This was never intended. Did I want them to have more decisive effects on each other than the non-violent plot allowed? Or did I dislike them in any case, and want to draw blood myself?

For I might add here that a year or two's work on a single novel is an inhuman trial for a creative artist. He must meet and deal with the same characters, day after day, month after month — though he is per-sistently fired with the need to express quite other personalities met with in his own life during that time. He can quite easily grow to hate such characters, though it is his duty to love them. He is in much the same position as that of the manager of a small residential hotel, who must deal with half a dozen regulars year after year. Perhaps he grows to love them? I very much doubt it. And that is one reason why I like to write short stories. One can concentrate inspiredly on a single theme or set of characters for a heightened fortnight, easily keeping up steam, seldom levelling off. But, alas, to write story after story after story for years is itself not aesthetically variable enough: the broader canvas beckons — and again one finds oneself in charge of another hotelful of ever-demanding residents.

In the airplane, the lady in the inked white dress is revealed as having a seductive foreign-ness, and as being dissatisfied with the holiday from which she is returning. The possibilities compound. And, along with more scenic detail of the general experience of flying, the two of them now share food 'like tried lovers'. Dunko feels they are becoming 'delightfully close, snuggly'.

Never before re-reading this story for this present book did I notice this word 'snuggly'. I was appalled. No such word exists. It should be snugly. It seems unbelievable, though here and now you must believe it, that this mistake has got through many, many stages of proof and different proof-readers. First me. In manuscript, and in typescript, and in printed proof sent to me by the magazine where it was first printed. Add, less blameworthy, the editorial proof-reader of the magazine and its printer's proof-reader. And then — all this all over again as it went into book-form, proofs sent to me, proofs checked in the publisher's and printer's offices. In this, I am far more to blame than the others, who might reasonably have thought that here is a crazy writer who coins words for his own purposes. If so, it was not consciously done. Though I see in retrospect that in its inaccurate way it works, the extra 'g' in the word infers 'cuddly' as well. I notice in the manuscript that there is no hesitation whatsoever about that second 'g'. Only a crossing out of an 'e' which had the word originally as 'snuggley'. This may give pause for thought to any student of philology and of the emergence of words from old manuscripts. If such a mistake can get through half-a-dozen trained minds in a supposedly efficient today, how much more must have bedevilled the language from the quill of a half-literate mediaeval clerk?

Now with Dunko and his red-white-and-blue half-Belgian holiday-frustrated consort, snugness turns to danger. The plane runs into an electric storm. A year or two before I had run into a black and bumpy storm over Norway, and the experience is re-invoked here. One or two parochial memories of my own nearly crept in but were finally discarded, like a grey-faced man with a black hat who sat rocklike throughout, though the colour of his face-rock turned from grey granite to chalk-white in five tremendous, tremulous minutes. Such a memory was discarded as too personal, and diversionary from the central action.

Meanwhile the experience of the storm has cemented their relationship by touch. But even while he holds her, Dunko has time to wonder about the red emergency exits. And the haphazard idea of queueing occurs to him — a minor though important touch to keep the mood not as serious as circumstances make it appear. The relationship, the mood must as yet be kept light — as it would be in real life.

Then the price of the dress comes up again, reminding us of an earlier *frisson* when Dunko worries about the cost of replacement. Mention of sums of money in a story is almost a sensual device. The purse is like a sixth sense. It always strikes an anxious note. But now with Dunko even this becomes submerged in his interest in her, now grown strong indeed.

And they arrive over London, with the warning note that Mrs Cabot lives far in the north and must spend the night in London. . . .

From the plain planting of this night she must spend alone in London, I think I must have decided, or the two characters had decided, that they must have an affair together. Yet the nature of any such affair is still a question mark for the reader.

And down they come, with a further scenic description from the air-traveller's viewpoint, both from an aerial view through the windows and from tactile moments within the aircraft — all evocative to readers who have flown. After, then, a crescendo as they descend, there comes an intentional dulling of the pace to match the dullness of arrival; to suggest, too, the possibility still that they might now part company. But not for more than a few lines — Mrs Cabot has now taken over the initiative, has turned temptress, and, as Dunko allows himself to be tempted, his guilt (and one hopes, the reader's) is put into big booming capital letters by the fatal sign, ominous, vaguely ridiculous, NO SMOKING ON THE APRON.

At this point it might be as well to ask what satisfies the writer most in the course of his writing. In my case, and beyond the major importances of character and action, what intrigues me most are similes, metaphors, freshly created turns of phrase and conceptions. Thus, I am stimulated when I find the hostess has 'a set toothpaste smile plastered where her mouth should have been'. And by the aerial view of the channel as 'far-below skin wrinkled on a grey old hand, with lost ships like scattered moles'. And by Dunko's feeling for the phrase 'wireless telegraphy' and all it means to him. These, it always seems to me, raise the experience above just looking or feeling to an immediate visionary level. The purist reader will dislike them. We differ. Though he has a point, perhaps, with certain possibly overblown images, as with that plane weaving about 'like a hook-mad barracuda'.

I was, and still am, unsure of this simile. It may be too wild even for so wild a predicament. I remember striving for something more exact, finding nothing and finally giving in. Naughty. And I excused its too evident tropicality and wateriness by telling myself that 'barracuda' has a vague feeling of aircraft about it, it is the kind of word with which aircraft are branded. Naughtier. It wavers on that fatal inexactness of a 'steamer cutting its way through the waves like a knife through butter' — butter is nothing like water. The only hope, still, with my barracuda is that its exoticism lightens the quality of that dramatic moment, which ought in this story to be strong but not grave.

I wonder too, whether the aircraft is not likened to too many other things within too short a space: a barracuda, a tube train, a cigar, after already being a moth. I suppose such different similes might occur in the mind of an alerted traveller; but this might be the kind of truth whose artifice needs artificially toning down.

Now with Dunko still guiltily fumbling, it is the porter — extraneous Fate — with the luggage who decides matters. This is workable. A quality of real life is the constant effect of outside influences on the supposedly free will of people. It is more acceptable, though, that the influence is slight, as with this porter — Dunko could still have withdrawn the baggage, had he really wanted to. To have had, for instance, Mrs Cabot in a sudden fainting fit, or something like that, would have rung too intense a bell.

In the now quickly accelerating cab Dunko accelerates matters by taking over from Fate and squeezing her knee, and later Mrs Cabot in return engineers him, though with fair reason still, up to her room — one remembers that they are still fellow-travellers, people in transit, and not quite governed by laws of normal decorum.

And by the way, what kind of people are they? Congenial, provident, middle-class, married — probably under middle-age, probably fairly attractive. No more. These are the facts beyond which their anonymity as travellers should not go. They are prototypes of what we know to be a fairly ordinary kind of passenger seen about air lounges. To be more particular would not have helped, would in fact have destroyed the facility with which the reader could identify his own experience. They could, and should be, anyone like themselves.

And now Dunko and Mrs Cabot have taken over the narrative, and are on their way to having an affair. Plainly nothing will now stop them. But there must still be hesitations on the way. The correct atmosphere of diffidence must be stated — thus the detail, the drinks, the feeling of the room and Dunko's final moment of sadness at so ununique a predicament — which in fact propels him to clinch matters and embrace her.

They act as human beings do, clinging to notions of propriety, yet at the same time going against them. 'No', she groans, drawing him closer. 'Blast', Dunko gasps before kissing her. It is easy, but not so easy.

Then they make love. And now, behind the scenes in the author's mind, a very odd matter indeed: that room — I can see it plainly now — was a room I knew in my childhood. It was not a hotel room, though

in appearance it well could have been. A rather badly, or at least neu-
trally furnished room in some seaside resort. I forget what happened
there, and why the impression should be so lasting. The dressing-table
was of varnished yellow wood, the bay window where it stood was not
curved but sharp-cornered in a triptych shape. Perhaps at some time
later in life, I myself had some strong emotional experience in a room
which reminded me of the childhood room? I do not know. It is all
forgotten, yet very clear in geography and essence.

And it is coupled with another memory from my childhood, with
the fact that the dying sunlight on the wall, the dead gold, comes from
a time when I was about ten years old and spent weeks in one room re-
covering from scarlet fever. It was a west-facing room, I grew inti-
mately to know the sadness of evening sunlight and I have never
forgotten it. And this must all be trebled by the use of the word
'peignor'. I remember that, at the time of writing, I was poised to
write the word 'kimono'. But that was certainly too old-fashioned.
Yet almost as old-fashioned a word was substituted. Why did I not
write 'house-coat' or 'dressing-gown', even 'robe'. Perhaps the peignoir
sounded more exotic, scented, silken: nevertheless, it was still a word
from childhood many years ago. So there we have it — a seduction
scene, the rearing up of sex, and the author back in the haze of his
childhood.

But when they have made love, 'the room seemed strangely empty'.
That has nothing to do with childhood. It is an adult attempt, from
experience, to state in a single economic and touching phrase a well-
known vacuum of the senses, depression after excitement. And then
they are ready to part. There is a last recapitulation of that earlier
phase of exchanging cards, like an echoing theme in music, and they
part. The duel was plainly over.

There must, though, be a coda. Dunko, the now absolutely guilty
Dunko, is still smudged with lipstick — shirt, suit. And the earlier problem of what his wife will say has not yet been resolved.

It must be. And here I have used what could be thought as a trick
ending. Partly it is. But it is also quite reasonable, and involves two
other important matters — the loving trust of his wife's reception,

bringing a shadow of shock to us who know of his infidelity only an hour or two before. And the second is a quality most important to all endings — the finality of the episode itself yet the implicit sense that thereafter life will continue. The people in the story should have lived — and must go on living. Here again there is a parallel in music — in the final stroke of the conductor's baton, the final chord of music, and that exquisite moment of silence, when time seems to expand limitlessly, before the great accolade of applause.

We seem to have two definitions of the ending of a book — happy and sad. One would propose another, overriding both states: the *round* ending.

An ending that truly "rounds off" the narrative, completing it as a broad and living thing — an egg, if you like, rather than a straight thin line between arbitrary points. Round indeed as the final chords of that symphony — whose quality is not only finality but also a balanced suggestion that the music really continues, and only 'stops' for the practical reason that the audience must go home. Thus with a story or novel — which deals with human beings who cannot all conveniently die — an ending must suggest the continuance of life, and, by definition, of that which makes life continuable and endurable, hope: the end must be a statement of beginning.

Too often an author takes exactly the opposite course — like a man running a race, seeing the end of one or two years' work, he careers faster and faster until the breathless moment when he passes the posts. But of course, there are no real posts, if his book has anything to do with life and is not just a plot; and it is at that very last moment that he should stop and take another breath, the deepest of all, for his problem is now to state Time. And today more than ever he must be careful of this — for the pace of writing is fast and breathless in it-self: shortened sentences, quicknesses, understatements all compound to deny the proper long rumbling sense of time slowly passing. 'Living happily ever after' was one of the first aesthetic realizations of what I mean — and is of course too questionable for us today.

'Happy' cannot stay without qualification, but the 'ever after' must remain valid, even if it contains no more than a trace of the hope that makes time bearable. That is why the endings of, say, *Madame Bovary* and of *The Cherry Orchard,* which are generally held to be 'sad', are in reality round and balanced and in a way hopeful. In the first there is death, disillusion and the decadence of fortune. But then, one must read into Emma's death the only possible happy release; and after that, Charles has a time of resignation, even of reconciliation with Rodolphe, before his own death. The fate of the child seems at first appalling, but then you realize that it *lives,* that a bad beginning does not mean perpetual servitude, that the Bovaries are in this slight way carried on; there is hope and continuance.

And with *The Cherry Orchard* the old house may have gone – but they are all off to a new life somewhere else. It would be very different if the curtain came down on everyone hanging about hopeless on the stage. Only Firs is left – and it is near the end of his life and he would not want to go.

These and so many others infer the passing of future time, not necessarily too pleasantly – at random take the quiet acceptance, not resignation, of *Esther Waters,* or the fine sense of continuance, not defeat, of Hemingway's *The Old Man and the Sea,* an exact statement that man may be defeated temporarily but never absolutely. The end is simply a beginning.

The manuscript and typescript pages illustrated here may now be looked at in close detail. It is easy to see on the manuscript what corrections were made during the flow or stutter of writing, and which others were made during my routine read-through a week or more later. The corrections occurring *on* the writing line were made during writing, anything above or inserted otherwise was made later. Exceptions to this occur in insertions on the line at the ends of lines where there was marginal space. My own method of writing is very close to the effect of stuttering in speech, stopping in mid-sentence to search for the exact word, crossing out one or perhaps two insufficient words on the way, perhaps rephrasing or inverting the whole sentence.

To ease the check-over a week or more later, I always leave wide margins on the manuscript for insertions: I say 'a week' later — this would be ideally a month or more later, so that one could approach the test the more clinically, nearer to the remove of an outside reader, and thus more capable of cutting parochial quirks which may have minced their way in; everyone is full of pet words, pet philosophizings, pet phantasms of the moment, and these should be dealt with severely.

But alas, such a month's removal is in practice difficult: one is curious about what has been written, too often the hand goes to the drawer and pulls out the manuscript sooner than later. There is, however, a second chance, when the typescript is done.

Nowadays one should avoid as far as possible the third chance, re-writing at proof stage. Formerly writers rewrote at length at proof stage: nowadays, setting costs are so high that the whole publishing economy would collapse if this were done. The purpose of proofs is now only to check printers' errors, or elide blatant inaccuracies on the author's part.

In practice, the first two chances of correction occur too quickly. However, if it happens otherwise, if a manuscript or typescript hangs about too long in your hands, the temptations to dicker with it might finally spoil the work. An artist can seldom leave his work alone. This is most obvious with a painter, who has a whole accusing canvas staring him in the eye: if it hangs about the studio too long he will forever be dabbing at it, and in the process perhaps eliminating his first and most important inspiration in the search for a further but now artificial effect. At least the writer has to turn back the grey pages: reading and writing are a mechanical process, not directly sensual, and the writer thus has an inherent safeguard — although faced with a single page, the pen will all too readily score out a word or two, add others. Good or bad? It is not easy to be sure. The alternatives are so many. Sometimes, though, instances are obvious: for example, I wrote a novel once with a Spanish background and began this not long after a long journey round Spain. It was too soon. That book is far too full of descriptions of Spanish landscapes, streets, houses, dress and other minutiae which drown the characters and the action. Re-reading it today, and if it were in typescript again, I would cut about a quarter of this descriptive matter, and, for once, be certain I was right.

With this present story, apart from altering certain words, toning down or up certain epithets, I would also be tempted to try larger changes: for instance, I have a feeling that on the last page I went too fast. Perhaps the man's exit from that hotel and his slow journey home should be described, together with a deeper dwelling on his sadness and guilt and his gathering of defences to face his wife. This could be moving, could also build up further suspense. Yet it would lose dramatic abruptness. Perhaps, then, just a line or two? I am still not sure.

On the whole, I am glad that the material publication of a story or book completes it, puts to it a 'that's that'. Usually the chances of embellishment are outweighed by the dangers of eliminating inspiration, and that most important factor, the unanalysable quality between the lines. That should be sacred indeed. And the author is no god, he can be humanly so close to the work that he can only see the trees, with the wood of his first purpose become invisible: he forgets it and remembers it, in fact takes it for granted. But to the reader the impact will be fresh and quite different. Also, at a lower level, the author may be simply in a fractious mood, or liverish, or just tired, when he is tempted to dabble with the thing again. He may be just bad-tempered and want to stab and cut at it. He should recognize such a mood and postpone the pen; but life is not so ideal. God protect all surgeons.

Ten pages of the manuscript have been selected here. Of their nature, they cannot be of world-shattering interest, but they do all illustrate different aspects of a run-of-the-mill process. So:

THE MANUSCRIPT

now a ~~mite~~ excited, a ~~slight~~ edgy, about this ~~place~~
woman in white who stood to his left and slightly
behind him. She was not pretty, but very attractive.
She was ~~very~~ smart, and smelled smart: ~~the~~
coloured hair and face, scent, silk, ~~washed leather~~ and soft leather
~~assured them~~ sparked out messages from
her. She stood armoured and sure, ~~probably~~
like an ~~old~~ actress, and dabbed last lipstick
on her lips.

Bates ~~smelled~~ smelled her, ~~and eyed him~~
~~stalked~~ dismissed her — for what had he, ~~happily~~
well-~~enough~~ married, to do with painted ladies in
aeroplanes? — and watched a ~~great large~~ fat silver jet-lin-
~~er~~ amble about with a blind look, ~~or with~~
the blind purpose of ~~like a large~~ a ~~scrawled~~ expectant metal moth looking
for somewhere for her eggs. Another plane
was whining high, a ~~spit~~ hoover offstage.
celestial And up swooped another low off the
ground, too low it looked — would it ever
gain healthy height? // It would. But
~~there~~ again, Dunko knew ~~all~~ about that too,
the greasy moment of taking off, the too
nonchalant glance down to ~~see~~ the trees &
roofs really had got smaller enough, the ~~whitewashed~~
sudden taste of the glucose sweet again,
the relief heaved. And he remembered his

MS PAGE 2

Line 1   A 'little' becomes 'mite', as a felicitous rhyme with 'excite'. In the typescript, it looked too much of a rhyme, and became 'little' again.

'At least' eliminated as unnecessary.

'Young' eliminated. Better to leave her age uncertain, thus to cover a larger class of imagined traveller.

Line 3   'him' added to solidify geography of scene.

Line 4   'Very' unnecessary. 'Colour' repeated in next line.

Line 5   'hair' erroneously left out. The sensuous immediacy of 'soft' preferred to the crossed out 'expensive'.

'Were her messages' eliminated as too flowery.

Line 6   'armoured her' also eliminated as inaccurate at this point: armour a defence, not an attack. Keep armoured effect till next line.

Line 7   'probably' out, as indecisive. She either had these 'actress' qualities or she had not.

Line 8   Pen stutter.

Line 10   'Watched' goes out, 'smelled' is more forceful, suggesting both her scent and him scenting her as a male.

'shrugged his shoulders' replaced by 'dismissed' as neater, more incisive.

Line 11   'happily' goes out in favour of 'nicely' in next line. But 'nicely' sounded too 'chatty', so the more embracing 'well' was put in as also suggestive that his marriage might by now be more a habitual than an elevating experience.

Line 13   'fat' more sensuously descriptive than 'large'.

'jet-liner' interpolated from next line for legibility for typist.

Line 14   'ample' a mistake for 'amble'. A mistake consequent upon mouthing words for euphony as one writes, and writing a shade too fast. (Thus often I find I might write 'right' for 'write'.)

Line 15   'the blind purpose of' is a later interpolation on read-through and introduced to strengthen the image, as also 'large' for 'grounded' and 'metal'.

Line 17   'celestial' again a later interpolation, a much better image and a visionary phrase. Incidentally, here we have the word 'hoover' over which I always pause. Hoover is a brand-name, which in fact has entered the language and now the appendix of the Oxford English Dictionary. The alternative, vacuum cleaner, is far too clumsy. And here, in relation to aircraft, there is the added inference of 'hover'.

Line 18   'yet' goes in for greater clarity.

MS PAGE 2 *continued*

Line 20   A new paragraph, a white breath for the eyes, is becoming more and more a necessity nowadays, with the accelerated pace of things in general and I would say certainly with readers reluctant to face too large a block of words with no relieving white space. Look at a page of Simenon, an economical writer with a fast narrative pace, and see how extremely short his paragraphs are, how seductive the whitened pages.

      But in this instance there is also a dramatic reason — to make the asseveration 'it would' more abrupt and thus definitive.

Lines 23, 24   Interpolation of 'that' and following simply a stronger form of the same phrase.

Lines 24   'relief heaved' relegated to a line later.

braced ~~taken~~

troubled. She was still working away with the lipstick, sucking her lips in, ~~standing~~ firmly ~~on high~~ [back] ~~too~~ heels. He went ~~once~~ once more over his preparations, passport, ~~ticket, docket~~ ticket, ~~flight docket~~, briefcase, ~~&~~ bag, ~~seat for flight~~ flight docket — and then remembered his fountain pen. He looked at the floor. ~~Rough carpet~~ No carpet. ~~And it's~~ A drop of ink wouldn't harm? // He took the pen out and uncapped it. Just as he pressed the lever, the door to the field was swung open, a great gust of salt Baltic air blew in, ~~and~~ the spilling ink was caught in mid-drop and blown sideways to ~~spraying~~ a rich blue tattoo all over ~~that~~ woman's white dress.

~~He~~ 'Aaah', she gasped, and her fine shoulders squared. 'You great clumsy idiot,' she gasped. 'You idiotic fool,' and at the same time she raised her hand to ~~say~~ mark her point, ~~and~~ jabbing him with it as she repeated, 'You'll pay, pay, pay for this...'

And she repeated it and it was the hand that held the lipstick that jabbed ~~it~~ him, all over his lapels, his shirt, and as high as his collar as her face

It always leaked under height pressure...

para

But

Splatter

— you

MS PAGE 4

Line 2   'braced' gives more the whole feeling of legs straightened back by high heels. 'back', ditto.

Line 3   'over his' transposed to allow added strength of 'once more'.

Lines 4, 5   Arrangement of items in best order, leading up to syllabic tattoo of 'flight docket', also emphasizing the idea of flight. Cut 'scent for Sheila' as being too chatty; also to reserve his wife's name for casual but more dramatic presence later.

Lines 7, 8   Inserted phrase for necessary information, logical reason for his action. Eliminated 'Rough concrete' and 'Hard stuff' because, as mentioned earlier, I was worried as to that floor and whether a man would really do this. Decided that an abrupt, almost disciplinary 'No carpet' was an adequate solution to this little problem of credibility.

Line 9   New paragraph here as more active for narrative purposes.

Line 10   'But' seemed necessary, announcing disaster.

Line 12   Do not know what that 'with' was going to do. But it probably intended a too graceful extension of the sentence: whereas short, sharp occurrences separated by breathless commas were what was needed for the violence of that small moment.

Line 14   As above. More active than splatter*ing*. 'Splatter' later on in the story becomes 'spatter' as the ink has dried — 'splatter' has a more liquid sound for the wet, wind-blown ink.

Line 16   'Ah' was too short, so 'Aaah'. It is a pity, I always think, that a person should still 'gasp'. It teeters on the cliché line. But perhaps it is a word so over-used by now that it has become a tradition, a cypher. However, it must be a fact that any writer who cares about the language spends half his writing time gnashing his teeth to find a way to use good and simple words freshly, unbogged by the former gross innocence of cliché. It is astounding how many simplicities have become unusable. For instance, 'She gave a gasp'.
People still do 'give gasps'. But the pen falters — for people have also gasped too much and too long. Then how about: 'drew in a short breath'? No, too many short breaths drawn. Then: 'took a short breath'? No. Not the same thing. And so on. And the writer, keyed up to an imaginative pitch perhaps difficult exactly to regain ever again, sits with his pen bogged on these simple technical problems of taking breaths, or, say, getting his characters emotionally about the room without the use of a wheeled cliché.

Read a modern who cares, a sensitive stylist like Scott Fitzgerald, and you will find, well disguised, the results of this struggle. In *Tender is the Night,* at the

MS PAGE 4 *continued*

moment of a kiss toward the end of the book, I am pleased to find a gasp. They kiss, and ' . . . she gasped half with passion for him, half with the sudden surprise of its force.' I will bet Nicole really just gasped, with no halves about it, and that the latter half was occasioned purely by Fitzgerald's own nervousness of the moment.

Line 17   Insert of extra 'you' to emphasize her breathlessness.

Line 20   'Instil' cut as too refined a word, 'mark' being much more forceful and implicitly suggesting that she was 'marking' him at the same time.
'and' cut for pace.

Line 25   'at' cut because it does not suggest actual touch.

he sat, not blaming two women; and the plane slightly ~~began the~~ shuddered as ~~it again~~ it slid ~~its after~~ smoothly off ~~down the~~ towards the runway.

The uneasy thought of a hundred pounds for a dress, ~~and the business of today. Perhaps the small clauses in his insurance policies~~ had to be put aside in consideration of ~~his~~ a greater loss, that of his wife. Yet Wives and husbands, assumably in each other's confidence, should surely be able to ~~discuss~~ discuss such an absurd story, and to laugh about it? But was there ~~was~~ not a ~~little~~ too ~~even~~ privately amused twist to his wife's lip as he stammered through the whole ridiculous rigmarole, and a certain half-light of fear in her eyes afterwards, when they had willingly laughed together about the whole thing? And in my case, surely the episode was a trifle too ridiculous to be quite believed? Damn life, he thought, that is made up so much of these trip-rope absurdities, rather than seriously heroic traps. Why couldn't he, just for once, be permitted to save someone from drowning?

The ~~pilot was~~ captain was ~~running his engines~~ running the plane around. ~~over against the~~

where ~~were these~~ were these ~~to ride~~ run-away horses ~~to~~ at whose heads to throw ~~himself~~ himself? Life the bloody banana ~~skin~~ skin, ~~said~~ he thought.

MS PAGE 8

Line 2	'began to' cut. This phrase is many a writer's weakness. It is sometimes necessary, but often denotes a hesitation not in the story but in the writer's mind itself. 'its engine slid it quite' cut as being far too clumsy.
Line 3	'along the' what? Possibly tarmac? Better to suggest the destined, and, of course, threatening runway itself.
Lines, 6, 7	'and the business of looking through the small clauses in his insurance policies' is cut because it sounds as dull as the small clauses themselves. Also, it leaves a shorter sentence where the two kinds of loss can be compared more directly.
Line 9	Insert 'Yet' to give the sentence more of a feel of self-question.
Line 11	Some word begun here, which was cut in favour of 'discuss', a word with an atmosphere of married couples.
Line 12	Insert 'to' for better prose value.
Line 13	Pen-stutter of 'was'. Elimination of 'little' — either she was privately amused or she was not. Cut 'amu' to allow 'privately'.
Line 14	Originally 'her' lip. Change to 'his wife's' for greater force and clarity.
Line 18	'whole absurd episode' cut because it echoes too closely on 'whole ridiculous rigmarole' above. 'thing' is a reasonably loose substitute because he is talking to himself in his mind.
Line 19	Insertion of 'quite' for emphasis; a case of a diminishing word having the opposite effect.
Line 24	Insert here to strengthen the concept. It was too short, too weak before. Now these images worry at him, reflect his flustering, as also does the final emphatic 'Life the bloody banana-skin'. 'He thought' added here to bring him up close to the thought, almost to make him speak it aloud.
Line 25	'captain' a more authoritative word than 'pilot'. 'roaring his engines' sounded incorrect here. Usually this is done later. Cut 'even inside the'. I do not know why, or what was intended.

miniature

cigar-shaped roomlet, like a tube-train ~~crossing~~ men within in a tunnel. Yet how much worse if ~~they all~~ all these

lights ~~they~~ had all gone out! Dunko massaged ~~his~~ his 17ᵗʰ Cabot and glanced efficiently up at the

(margin: opposite the next seat along)

red-marked emergency exit — but how in the devil to ~~q~~ open it? ~~and~~ Push what? And how to get round in front of the two people sitting ~~as first~~ there? What ~~did~~ one do — ~~crossed out~~

'There!' he said, as they zoomed out into pure blue daylight.

(margin: stiffen the upper lip and queue?)

'Oh God,' she said, straightening herself up and withdrawing her hand quite sharply.

(margin: having been / Aim to see)

~~...~~ She was offended ~~to see~~ with him for ~~lack of control. As had for~~ her own lack of control. But this passed. ~~...~~ the stronger fact of bodily contact, the intimacy of aeroplanes, ~~so~~

in its condensed way

the escapade of ~~journey~~ voyage — for a 'plane-trip ~~crossed out~~ had the liberalising effect on the romance strings of a ~~crossed out~~ sea-voyage — these brought them closer together, so that ~~their~~ their knees were touching and

murmuring

he was ~~...~~ without shame such compliments as 'your lapis lazuli eyes'. ~~...~~ Flirting had ~~...~~ given way to something ~~...~~ far

(margin: fleshier)

fleshier ~~...~~, ~~...~~ even heartfelt: ~~Dunko~~ and Dunko had quite forgotten his earlier reservations,

MS PAGE 19

Line 1	A difficult stutter on 'crashing tube-train'. All too grandiose. Insert of 'miniature' to match the airplane's lighter structure. Cut mark of interrogation, first intended as question in Dunko's mind.
Line 2	Forgot to mention 'lights', thus insert.
Line 3	Cut 'the woman' as too much like a joint of meat. Substitution of 'his Mrs Cabot' as being appositely intimate yet correct.
Line 5	'opposite the next seat along' inserted for exact setting of scene.
Line 6	Pen-stutters.
Line 7	Ditto. Cut repetition of 'in front'.
Line 8	Insert to strengthen the concept, in the same manner as insert in Page 8, line 24.
Line 13	'At first' slightly slowed it up. Better the direct contrast of her offended feeling.
Lines 13, 14	Insertion of him seeing her lack of control gives a truer meaning.
Line 15	Cut 'And' as fussy.
Line 16	Substitute comma for the line punctuation, because a line comes a little later and too near.
Line 17	Cut 'journey' as being too suggestive of travel down on the earth; 'voyage' more dramatic, and heralding the explicit reference to sea voyage. In passing, I would nowadays try to remember to cut those hyphens in 'plane-trip' and 'sea-voyage'. They serve no purpose. Generally, the Americans are better at dispensing with the hyphen than the English; to their credit they have cut them to a minimal necessity. I see also that the apostrophe before 'plane in the MS disappears in the text — at least this antiquated fussiness was got rid of.
Line 18	Cut 'was a condensed' and insert a neater placement in the line above.
Line 19	Ditto, cut 'condensed'.
Line 21	Cut 'their' to allow for 'soon'.
Line 22	'murmuring' suits the moment better than the eliminated 'saying'.
Lines 23, 24	Pen-stutters. I wish now I had stuttered more on that 'lapis lazul eyes', and scrubbed it out. It is far too flowery a joke for such a man; affected, literary, a private giggle in any case.
Lines 25, 26	'much more fleshly' is rightly cut as being too flowery, like the above. Apparently the surgical knife is not consistent. 'hearty' becomes the suitably ironical 'even heartfelt'. But in the typescript it is to

MS PAGE 19 *continued*

go out altogether as both superfluous and wrongly felt.
'Dunko' was too staccato, needed an 'and'.

21

But

When she went to wash her hands', he was left for a moment with thoughts of his own predicament, and his own felt guiltily empty. Then as she was back, there and lively in the flesh and he felt hot and handsome as before. The guilty memory of Sheila dovetailing into 17th Cabot that they were both of the same colouring, two editions as it were of the same thing, and he felt both more betraying and more faithful at the same time.

By the time the captain was telling 'them they were passing over the English coast and on time, knew a superficial lot about each other, where they lived & what they liked. She did not comment on her husband, she simply kept off the subject. So did he, of his own.

But she lived in Cumberland, and had to spend the night in London....

They peered down at the very green plan of London beneath — it seemed to be a clean & freshbuilt garden city — and then went out, the seat-belts
(the no-smoking sign lit up)

[margin note:] and of his wife,

[margin note:] made him notice

[margin note:] Drunko and 17th Cabot

MS PAGE 21

Line 1   Cut 'They' because whole approach was re-thought. This was probably at the beginning of a day's work.

Line 2   Insert cut. No idea why or what.

Line 3   A necessary insert to remind us of reasons for his guilt. 'Wife', not her first name, is used because 'Sheila' must be used sparingly. I dislike too many first names. They seem to destroy the seriousness and authority of the prose, bringing it down to the level of those broadcast panel-games where people who hardly know each other address each other loosely, with a dreadful false chumminess, by these first names. Also, the first name is a province of the pot-boiling magazine story. It may be argued that the immediate use of first names between people has become a growing social habit today, and that this is an honourable attempt to allow for easier and closer communication between people. I wonder. And I do not think such a technique necessarily invites the reader closer to the characters. Closer in a superficial way, perhaps: but not in the right way. Personalities are cheapened. Conversely, the first name is sometimes necessary with one or other of the characters who must themselves be conversationally affable, in fact like the Dunko in this particular story. Otherwise, the habitual use becomes as false as the habitual use of 'darling' and 'love' among theatrical people.

Line 4   'but as soon' cut for economy, her more direct entrance preferred. The 'as' goes in printing, left in here in error.

Line 5   'carefree and (something)' cut as novelese word.

Line 6   Pen-stutter.
'Only he just' cut; that use of only is very often suspect as too talkative. 'Though', though not good, is more reliable. At least it often avoids the use of a cumbersome and almost now antiquated 'however'.

Line 7   'vision' is replaced by 'guilty memory', 'vision' being too elevated a word for this predicament. Also, the good word 'guilt' is drummed home again.
'Sheila': here it seemed necessary to bring the wife closer, having established the remote solidity of her presence earlier.

Line 8   'did jerk the realization' cut as clumsy.

Line 10   'oddly this' cut as too conspiratorial.

Line 15   Insert names for greater presence, and a kind of spotlighting of them together in an advanced relationship.
'lot ab', cut to allow for 'superficial'.

MS PAGE 21 *continued*

Line 17 Cut 'run down' as too strong an attitude for her. Mrs. Cabot must be kept pleasant: even if she does *not* run down her husband, the words 'run down' are there — as if they had occurred to her. The negative can often be dangerous on the page: 'not' is a little word compared with usually the longer, more vivid statement negated. Mud sticks.

Line 21 'was going to' cut as being less decisive than the dictated 'had'.

Line 25 'tremendously' cut as an over-used conversational adverb.

Line 26 'the cigarette went out' cut for the more visual aircraft sign, bringing one into the atmosphere of the aircraft again.

went on, and the runway came up to meet them. As always, Dinko averted his eyes from this. And this time He used the occasion to stare long and fixedly into hers. Then — brumpety-bump went the wonderful rubber wheels, they whizzed smooth along, and the engines at last reversed. It was the moment of safety. 'Ah', he said, with a look of pleasure. She took this to mean relief at a journey, their journey together, ended — and such a small sign of his interest ending help to accelerate in her

an idle thought, a wish, an idea. The idea became, vaguely, a decision.

Landings, arrivals ... no night richness of a city of red & yellow jewels beneath, no mystery of blue lamps studding like magic marsh-gas the barren flat dark field — no, here was simply London air in daylight, stale inland air after the salt breezes of Denmark. In the aircraft they shuffled among coats & hangers and in the thick silence left by the engine's last pop; Then endured the frank-eyed goodbyes of the hostess & steward, so attendedly personal as to be thoroughly inhuman; stepped down the stairs marvelling again at the size of the now so quiet big beast that had carried them so far — it

MS PAGE 22

Line 1	Pen-stutter.
Line 3	'And this time' inserted for emphasis. Pen-stutter on cut 'a'.
Line 4	Pen-stutter.
Line 5	Cut 'along' to allow smooth'. I used the adjective 'smooth' here instead of the adverb 'smoothly' because it is a smoother word.
Line 7	" 'Ah,' he said' " postponed for emphasis on 'the moment of safety' statement.
Line 8	'glance' cut – he was probably going to glance at her. A general 'look' glows more from inside him.
Line 9	Pen-stutter. But also indecision as to whether it was that particular journey or, as must be, all journeys.
Line 10	'this brief' cut for complete rephrasing.
Line 11	'accelerated' cut to introduce the slower, more casual 'help to', which of course should be 'helped to'.
Line 12	Insert to emphasize the idly slow occurrence of the idea to her; written with a rhythm to watch such a slow emergence.
Line 13	'mystery' is cut as inexact.
Line 14	'jewelled' cut as a cliché combined with 'city'.
Line 15	'goblin' cut because it was used in reference to their food earlier. Although a long way back, the word seemed dangerously insistent.
Line 16	'fairy' cut. A word of too airy a connotation.
Line 18	Insert 'salt' for clearer comparison.
Line 19	'Copenhagen' cut, because it is a large city with a fair amount of traffic and stale air. 'Denmark' is wider and breezier. Cut 'They'. Revision of approach.
Lines 19, 20	Cut 'rose' and insert 'shuffled up' as more descriptive.
Line 20	'Stale' cut in favour of 'thick', as being nearer to the sensation.
Line 21	'after' cut for clumsiness. Insert of 'they' – the sentence was getting too long for its purpose, which was a 'pop', a stop.
Line 22	'staring straight' cut as too inimical in feeling.
Line 23	Insert 'intendedly' to infer artificiality. 'To er' cut for some forgotten reason.

MS PAGE 22 *continued*

Line 24   'absolutely' cut as being too strong for such a minor moment. Substitution of a
more casual 'thoroughly' inserted in line above.

was neither sweating, nor puffing ~~heavy breathing~~ —
and walked together among other passengers
clutching their duty-free packages towards the
big solid ^brick^ airport building. ~~They a th~~ Isolated
on the broad field ~~they~~ the trailing little group wound
~~behind~~ like a ~~forlorn~~ ^lonely^ funeral party escaping
from their own coffin.

'Within ————— Walking distance!' he found himself saying.
'Lucky we didn't have to get one of those awful
tarmac buses. They're awful, those awful buses,
after you've come so far so quick.'

pura   ~~At th~~ She touched his arm tenderly and
smiled her strong smile. // 'Are you taking
the other bus, up to the terminal?' she asked.

pura   // He nodded, ~~as she ca~~ as she continued: 'My
hotel's ~~nearby~~ just by ~~the ~~ ^taxi^ I'll make
a bargain, if you ~~drop~~ ^take^ me there, I'll give
you a drink. Fair?' she proposed brightly, as
into ^it^ good clean fun.

As ~~she said this~~, he saw across her
shoulder a big notice: NO SMOKING ON THE
APRON

'Fair?' he laughed. 'It's dyed-in-the-wool
blonde. let's wash it in beer!' // Phew! And
pura   with that notice rumbling at him! And what
if the apron smokes on you, Drunko ^?^-boy?

MS PAGE 23

Line 1	'heavy breaths!' cut as sounding too excitable, too chatty.
Line 4	Insert 'brick' to visualize the building better, to emphasize its solid structure. Pen-stutter.
Line 5	Cut 'they', with more exact substitution of subject.
Line 6	Cut 'looked' as being less direct than the verb 'wound' inserted in Line 5. Cut 'forlorn' as a wrong use of alliteration, the funeral note being too sad for this.
Line 8	'Within' inserted to be more exact.
Line 12	Cut 'And' for rephrasing.
Line 13	New paragraph for isolation of dialogue lines.
Line 15	Ditto. 'she cont' cut for postponement after 'as'.
Line 16	Cut 'nearby'. Not really necessary, but the substituted 'just by' is a shade more as might be spoken. Cut 'she said' as not needed here.
Line 17	Cut 'drop' for insertion of the new visualized fact of a taxi.
Line 19	Cut 'at', 'with' being correct grammatically.
Line 21	No cut — but I feel there might well have been. It would probably be better if the NO SMOKING etc. notice were relegated to lower case lettering. This run of capital letters destroys the good look of the printed page. There is little reason why the notice should not enter within the usual prose confine. It was a case of the dramatist manqué getting out of hand. Usually I am careful to keep the page as orderly as possible — for instance in using always single quotation marks as against double ones looking too fussy, itchy.
Line 24	Cut exclamation mark. Arbitrary. But better gone as another follows. New paragraph to isolate preceding spoken sentence.
Line 25	Exclamation mark inserted to shorten sentence for better attack.
Line 26	'-boy' inserted after Dunko to suggest he is talking to himself as an affably admonitory companion.

and if set, set on what. So he went to the mirror,
and combed his hair with
his fingers.

'Drink!' she said, handing him a glass.
'There's more on the tray — only set, the two 'ticks in the bathroom, Get this blotter off my back.'

She came back not in another dress
but a peignoir.

They drank. Then, having so far
fixed the material scene, she
advanced no further. The swept off his
feet by so sudden and apparently
brazen a succession of events — taxi, lift,
shut door, drinks, peignoir — he found himself
expected to put his best
foot forward.

Daylight came grey through the window;
but golden whisky made night-light
inside him. And all around was the excitation
of unfamiliar feminine scents and objects —
she had already emptied a leather case
of cosmetics & bottles out into the dressing-table.
All this made for terrible silences. Once
they both started talking together; and
broke into laughter at this. But the laughter

MS PAGE 26

Line 1	Indecision. Confused by three 'too's' in a row.
Line 2	'Smoking heavily' cut as too obvious a back-reference to the apron.
Line 3	'brushed' cut for 'comb', plainly necessary with his fingers.
Lines 5, 6	'I'm just going into the bathroom' cut as too stilted.
Line 7	'get this blott' cut to make two sentences; short sentences are better in dialogue. 'of yours' inserted for definition.
Line 8	A stuttering of 'Buts', in and out, finally in.
Line 9	No cut — but notice that there is no pen-stutter on the use of the word 'peignoir'. (cf page 58)
Line 10	'But now' cut to make sense of sentence more direct, exact, with a 'Then'.
Line 11	Ditto, change from 'situation' to 'material scene'.
Lines 12, 13	We enter cliched metaphorland. Out goes the wind-sail metaphor as being too remote, sensually, from this reality. But a close-runner, 'swept off his feet' is allowed in. Probably I wanted a fairly valid conversational phrase after the preceding very formal 'advanced no further'.
Line 13	Pen-stutter.
Line 16	Cut 'to make a move' for a further conversational metaphor. This is nearly capped by a play on the metaphor, too self-conscious and luckily eliminated: 'But his best foot was'.
Line 17	Pen-stutter.
Line 18	The word 'beautiful' seems to have started here. Cut for the more closely sensuous colour of the drink.
Line 21	Cut 'strange' as being too exotic. The curtness of 'unfamiliar' softened by its hidden alliteration with feminine, seemed better suited. Cut 'smells' as being ambiguous, 'scents' safer.
Line 22	Cut 'box' for substitution of 'leather case' as a more luxurious object.
Line 23	Insert 'and bottles' as a factual necessity. Cut 'And' as an unnecessary smoothener. Better the abrupt nothing.
Line 24	Pen-stutter.
Lines 25, 26	Cut 'roared with' as being altogether too jolly.

was too loud, hysterical, and only emphasized the next patch of silence.

He looked at her, and felt suddenly sad. It seemed both exciting and pathetic. Rooms, rooms, men and women everywhere, all doing the same kind of thing. Each unique, each the same.

'Blast it', he gasped, and took her in his arms and kissed her for a long dark time. 'No', she groaned, 'no, no', and hugged him closer. The peignoir slid apart and they lay back on the bed and made love, while occasionally voices passed muffled in the corridor outside and a sound of plates washing echoed up from the kitchens far below the window, and the sun, far above in the sky wheeled lower and lower until just before its landing it shone low through the window and turned the wallpaper to dying, dead gold.

He got up and opened his own little flask of duty-free whisky and poured two drinks. They sat on the edge of the bed and drank,

MS PAGE 27

Line 1   Cut 'A roar' for above reason.

Line 2   Cut 'a new (sadness?)'. Arbitrary. I preferred to keep the image of sound/silence concrete.

'that came after' cut as superfluous, it could not come before. Insert 'the next' in previous line.

Line 4   Cut 'all so' and 'yet so' as either a weary drawl, or just lazy. The sentence stiffened by severity of 'both'/'and'.

Line 6   Cut 'Yet' as again too conversational.

Line 7   Cut 'so much' ditto. The phrase coos.

Line 8   Cut 'Damn', substitute 'Blast'. Why? This introduces the whole question of expletives and changes of usage. Fashions today change far more rapidly than in the past: the media of communication daily send forth such an increased barrage of words that they become more quickly over-used than ever before, losing in this process their proper emphasis. Obviously this affects vogue-words more than any other. A recent example is the change from 'with-it' to 'latched-on' to 'switched-on' (which gets mixed up with drug-intoxication) to etc., etc. Vogue-words of more complicated meaning join in, like cybernetics and eponymous and ecology, and though these do not lose their significance they do irritate by their self-conscious manner and thus in a different way lose power.

The writer had better avoid all such words as being too dangerous. There are always alternatives to hand.

But writers are in deeper trouble with material fashions, such as clothes and cosmetics, which change now very rapidly: here the alternatives are not to hand, they are in the unforeseeable future which will become the present when, say two years after writing, a work is finally published — and in these terms passé. To be passé is deflating, it has no period value, one must wait thirty years for that. It is a sad truth that today any detailed a description of a young person's clothes is dangerous and to be avoided.

Expletives change more slowly. But their power fluctuates. We all know the celebrated case of Shaw's introduction of a hitherto tabu two-syllable expletive in *Pygmalion*. That was in 1912. Yet the word still has some force. Since then other much stronger tabu-words have become publishable in some media, though still not in others. We are not yet free to swear as we like in print; we may in books, but not in some newspapers; we may on the stage, but not on most film and television screens. Such limits infer a graduation of lesser expletives beneath them.

MS PAGE 27 *continued*

What in fact is most emphatic must be left to the taste of the writer. For a long time, perhaps still, when I wanted to have a character be particularly unpleasant, I had him use the phrase: 'Sod you'. It seemed to me not over-used, and unpleasant in itself, less in its true meaning than in its hissing 's' and its echo of the word God. Yet I can see that it may not sound so strong to others. Similarly, in the case under discussion, 'Damn' seemed to me to have been weakened by an everyday use; 'Blast' is also weakened, but has inherent in it a more explosive sound and meaning.

Cut 'hugged' as too cosy.

Line 9   Cut 'round her', ditto.

Line 10   Cut 'no, no'. Too many no's would suggest something like an early film heroine flickering away into a bog of bathos.

Line 11   Here 'hugged', after the initially more formal 'took her in his arms' seemed reasonable. 'drew him closer' would have sounded too staid.

Cut 'to her' as superfluous. Who else was he hugged closer to?

Cut 'and her' in favour of beginning a new sentence which cuts the camera-eye away from their closeness to view them in greater solitudes of space and time.

Also because the sentence will be long, to match in cadence the long passing of time.

Lines 12, 13   Thus, as above, 'The' takes on a capital letter and 'love' takes on a comma. The
14, 15   statement 'for a long time' is cut to allow the length of the sentence later to imply this. And 'until the dead gold sun came on the wall (burn?)' is cut for postponement until the end of the sentence, for with its dying light and sensation of sad ending it is a symbol of the end of love-making.

Line 16   Cut 'echoed in' because it is not so accurate as 'passed muffled', and also because 'echoed' will be needed for the echo from the hotel well.

Line 17   Cut 'crane'. There was to be a sound of building machinery here: but the more intimate sounds of plates being washed were closer to the room — correctly it should be 'being' washed, because plates do not wash themselves, but I used the wetter suggestion of 'washing about'. (Also, that sound of washing-up, beside being a sound descriptive of inner hotel rooms, again seems suspiciously close to childhood, in the sense questioned back on page 57).

Cut 'crockery' as being not so immediately sensational as 'plates'.

Cut 'came', which would have been followed by 'echoing' as weaker than the peremptory past definite tense.

MS PAGE 27 *continued*

Line 19   Cut 'Far' to increase length of sentence.
             Cut comma after 'sun' for the same reason.

Line 21   Cut 'turned the wall' to postpone until after the description of how the light shone.

Line 24   Cut 'the' and insert 'his own' to suggest that Dunko is not doing all the taking, that this is altogether a shared experience.

In passing, one may note here a fashion change. Since 1961, when the story was written, the English customs have allowed a larger bottle as a duty-free concession.

and said so in
mutual consolation

talking a little too brightly, laughing, but ~~they~~
kissing no more. ~~They were both the Both after, they~~
~~both felt sad.~~ They ~~were~~ both ~~said~~ felt sad, and
the room strangely empty.

~~Later, but a little~~ Not much later, he said
goodbye. They ~~both~~ still had each other's cards, but
the duel ~~had been fought~~ ~~was~~ plainly over: ~~they~~ their goodbye
was ~~really~~ final ~~one~~.

He was home.
She ran to him, all brightness like a
big little dog, and hugged and hugged him, kissed
and kissed, ~~stroking~~ snuggling and snuffling,
stroking his ~~with her~~ chest with her soft cheek.
~~By~~ 'Oh darling, darling, darling!' ~~~~ Oh darling
~~look~~ what a mess I've made of you!'

filthy

para
// And then:

MS PAGE 28

Line 1	Cut 'now' as superfluous.
Lines, 2, 3	Indecision as to whether they should 'be' sad or 'feel' sad. 'feel' won.
Line 5	Cut 'later' and alternative 'only a little' as too kind. The moment must be rather harsh. 'Not much later' seemed to make the point. At a later stage, I relented and 'a little later' went back.
Line 6	Cut 'both' as superfluous, if 'each other's' must follow. Insert 'still'.
	Insert 'and said so in mutual consolation' to infer the sense of a quite remote politeness which can follow a love affair, and also to invoke a sad feeling of consoling each other.
Line 7	Cut 'had been fought' as too strong. It was never really fought. It was more a duet than a duel, although duet with its too musical connotation could not be used.
	Cut 'they' which would have been followed by them 'saying goodbye'. The change to 'their' followed by the noun is a straighter statement of a hard fact.
Line 8	Cut 'real' in favour of the plainly more final 'final'.
	In general, it can be helpful to allow words like 'final' or 'end' or 'ultimate' to slip unobtrusively into the last sentences of a story. They can add mass to the orchestration. Yet I find in the typescript that the whole final sentence is cut. Why? Probably because neither of them knew it was exactly final.
Line 14	Cut 'snuffling' to postpone until after snuggling.
Line 15	Cut 'with her' to postpone until after 'chest', the introduction of which makes for greater intimacy.
Line 16	New paragraph for greater dramatic effect.
Line 17	Cut 'look'. Arbitrary.
	Insert 'filthy' to refer to lipstick. This was seen later not to be enough. It was made much clearer by additions on the typescript.

THE TYPESCRIPT

This introduces the typescript, several pages of which are reproduced here, and upon whose obvious corrections I may as well comment for the record.

Thus, as with the page just mentioned, the word 'filthy' was at one point cut. And yet it appeared in proof-form — I probably telephoned the editor to re-insert it. Otherwise the insertion of references to his shirt and his suit now remind us of the lipstick marks, and the final 'beast' becomes heavily and sadly ironic.

By ending at this point, the writer hopefully leaves the reader considering the burden of guilt which Dunko will now have silently to bear for perhaps a long time; and this should create the correct illusion of life continuing long after the end of the page.

plane. And there it was again - he had superstitiously

to swallow the thought 'chance my luck on a plane,' just

as earlier he had nearly cancelled the phrase 'hope arrive.'

Whatever the statistics said about fewer accidents by

plane than by any other form of transport, the whole

horrible business still turned him up. Boasting aloud

to people 'I'm dead scared of the whole business' did

no good either. Every time he went up, until he was

right up, he walked out on the apron as with a halter

round his neck, fatal, surrendered, ticketed, and docketed

and no way out doomed. The other passengers were no help -

they easily assumed the appearance of unsentient cattle

herded witless to their doom fate. And the fixed knowing

smiles of the hostess and steward were false as a

nurse's death-cheer.

The woman in white did not seem so troubled. She

was still working away with the lipstick, sucking her

lips in, legs braced firmly back on high heels. He

went once more over his preparations, passport, ticket,

briefcase, bag, flight docket - and then remembered his

fountain pen. It always leaked under height pressure.

He looked at the floor. No carpet. A drop of ink

wouldn't harm?

TS PAGE 3

Line 2	Italics to emphasize the point of his thought.
Line 3	Ditto.
Lines 10, 11	Cut 'and' and replace 'no way out' with 'doomed' to make a more final phrase to the sentence, solidified further with the alliterative 'do's'.
Line 12	The incorrect word 'unsentient' overlooked until picked up at proof stage and altered to 'insentient'.
Line 13	Cut 'down' as now too closely repetitive.

4

He took the pen out and uncapped it. But just as
he pressed the lever, the door to the field was swung
open, a great gust of salt Baltic air blew in, the
spitting ink was caught in mid-drop and blown sideways
to splatter a rich blue tattoo all over that woman's
white dress.

'Aaah,' she gasped. and Her fine shoulders squared: *para*
'You - you great - clumsy - idiot,' she gasped, 'You
idiotic fool.' And At the same time she raised her   *para*
hand to mark her point, jabbing him with it as she
repeated, 'You'll pay, pay, pay for this. . .'

And she repeated it and it was the hand that held
the lipstick that jabbed him, all over his lapels, his
shirt, and as high as his collar as her face reached up
close to his. 'Aaah,' she sighed, at last receding,
while he stammered apologies.

Then: 'I say,' he said, 'I mean, really,' as he
looked down at his shirt and suit now daubed with red.

So there they stood, panting for breath and words,
the two of them red white and blue as a drunkard's eye.

But just then the door was officially opened, an
official chanted once again the flight number and beckoned
them out to the apron, and there they had to go.

TS PAGE 4

Lines 7, 9   New paragraphs to isolate speech.

might think ~~either~~. So there he sat, not blaming two

women; and the plane ~~s~~lightly shuddered as it slid

smoothly off towards the runway.

The uneasy thought of a hundred pounds for a dress

had to be put aside in consideration of a greater loss,

that of his wife. Yet wives and husbands, assumably in

each other's confidence, should surely be able to discuss

~~such~~ _{So} absurd/^astory, and to laugh about it? But was

there not a too privately amused twist to his wife's

lips as he stammered through the whole ridiculous

rigmarole, and a certain half-light of fear in her eyes

afterwards, when they had (hollowly) laughed together about

the whole thing? And in ^{an}~~my~~ case, surely the episode

italics was a trifle too ridiculous to be quite believed? Damn

life, he thought, that is made up so much of these trip-

rope absurdities, rather than seriously heroic traps.

Why couldn't he, just for once, be permitted to save

someone from drowning? Where were the run-away horses

at whose heads to throw himself? Life the bloody banana-

skin, he thought.

The captain was turning the plane around, *The*

~~was like being in~~ a big blind-moth stumbling about a

~~windy billiards table.~~ *A*nd as at other times Dunko

TS PAGE 7

Line 1   Cut 'either' as both superfluous and too conversational.

Line 2   Typescript revealed more clearly the reiterated s's in 'slightly', 'shuddered', 'slid' and 'smoothly'. One too many. Cut then 'slightly' for 'lightly', better in any case.

Line 8   MS has incorrectly 'such absurd'. Typist plainly confused. The phrasing of 'so' and 'a' more euphonious.

Line 12   Transfer 'hollowly' for cadence.

Line 13   Typing error.

Line 14   Italics for emphasis, I think now unnecessary. Italics of this kind are always best avoided.

Line 22   When the editor of *London Magazine* accepted the story, his only criticism was that the 'blind moth' simile was used twice. I thought he was quite right; and so cut this second reference.

daylight.

'Oh God,' she said, straightening herself up and withdrawing her hand quite sharply.

She was offended with him for having been there to ~~see~~ witness her ~~own~~ lack of control. But this passed, the stronger fact of bodily contact, the intimacy of aeroplanes, the escapade of voyage - for in its condensed way, a 'plane-trip had the liberalising effect on the romance strings of a sea-voyage - these brought them closer together, so that soon their knees were touching and he was murmuring without shame such ~~compliments~~ sweet everythings as 'your lapis lazul eyes.' Flirting had given way to something far fleshier; ~~even heartfeltz~~ and Dunko had quite forgotten his earlier reservations, as success took its exhilirating toll.

'I'm _so_ glad we caught fire,' he chuckled.

'What? We _didn't!_'

'I mean, when we began, remember? Along the wing? Otherwise you'd still have been at me over your dress, confess!'

She laughed. 'Oh that,' she said, ink-blue eyes lowered onto ink-stains.

'Where did you get it?' he asked. 'It looks so

TS PAGE 18

Line 5   Cut 'see' and substitute the stronger, more accusatory 'witness'.
Cut 'own' as superfluous.
Insert a comma after 'passed' to link the passing of her feeling with the reasons for that passing.

Line 11   Cut 'compliments'. Something more expressive was needed here. So, after a search, in went an appropriate 'sweet everythings'.

Line 13   Cut 'and heartfelt' as superfluous, and probably wrongly felt in any case.

Line 15   The mis-spelling of 'exhilarating' was missed but appeared correctly in the proof.

with all time hanging about slow as a fog after the fleet
concertinaed minutes of aluminium flight. Along with
these immediate sensations, his real responsible and
equally real delinquent sides fought for place. After
all - it was only for a drink? And time did not press?

So he stood at the terminal, fiddling. Fiddling
in his mind: and his pockets too. Should one throw
what ticket, what label away? Aeroplanes left one's
pockets full of paper. He stood fiddling, and meanwhile
two taxis had drawn up. Not asking, the porter put
both their luggages into the first taxi, and she said:
'Gaylor's Hotel, off the Cromwell Road there,' so that
who could blame him for not expostulating, rearranging,
goodbying - and with the queue behind for other taxis?
Who? He well knew who.

But now also the body came to help these mental
worries, old some said it said he wanted a drink and - as this
very thought rose to mind, conscious and alert, Dunko
squeezed her knee in the cab jerking and buzzing not
at all slowly toward Gaylor's.

He went to choose a table for them in the lounge
while she signed the register. But she interrupted,
looked round the big room with a BRRR sound and a shiver,   l.c.

TS PAGE 23

Line 1	Cut 'a' as clumsy.
Lines 1, 2	The idea of 'concertinaed' seemed ambiguous, sensually wrong, as if the aircraft were crushed. Better cut it, and thus insert 'fleet', which pleasantly echoed the following 'flight'.
Line 4	Typing error.
Line 12	Typing error.
Line 17	Cut the affected 'old soma said' and replace with 'it said'.
Line 20	Typing error.
Line 23	Lower case for BRRR as too aggressive on the page in capital letters.

laughing, but kissing no more. They both felt sad,

and the room _seemed_ strangely empty.

A little Not much later, he said goodbye. They still had

each other's cards, and said so in mutual consolation,

but the duel was plainly over: their goodbye was _&_

final. _then_

He was home.

She ran to him, all brightness like a big little

dog, and hugged and hugged him, kissed and kissed,

snuggling and snuffling, stroking his chest with her

soft cheek.

'Oh darling, darling, darling!'

And then: 'Oh _darling_ what a ~~bloody~~ mess I've made

of you _&_ ... _your shirt_ ... _your suit_ ... _oh Dunk & what_
a **beast** I am*...'

TS PAGE 26

Line 2 'seemed' was left out in the manuscript.

Line 3 'Not much' was after all too harsh. 'A little' was kinder.

Lines 5, 6 Cut 'a' and 'one', and the 'final' becomes more final.

Lines 13, Already commented upon.
14, 15

Now the typescript is ready for envelope and editor. In the time it takes, comes rejection or acceptance, and if the latter then later a proof. There is a time lapse of usually several weeks, so that the galley proof arrives for the writer's far more clinical eye.

In this case there were a number of small corrections, and one major one. As noted before, one must today keep such corrections down to a minimum, for they are very costly: the attitude is severely one of correction of mistakes, not of rewriting. But in this case the first paragraph dictated a most necessary change. After 'glass door' I had written 'marked in Danish *sjuv* (shove) and (through which etc.)'. I saw now that a foreign word coming so early, just when one was inviting the reader's first interest, spelled danger indeed: it might hold him up at this most precarious moment. Also, here was almost a private joke — *sjuv* being so like our slangish 'shove' — and this was not the place for it. Also, of narrative importance, was the fact that the door was kept then closed. This had to be stated. So the phrase became simply: 'still officially closed but'.

Smaller alterations included, for instance, trouble with the word tricolore — I had earlier written it, absent-mindedly, as 'tricouleur'; a cutting of the epithet 'ascendant' against 'bloodrush' (Page 33, line 14 and page 36, line 20) as too literary-sounding; a cutting of 'off his own' after 'So did he' (Page 36, line 35 of the text) as making for neater sense; and a last elimination of that final goodbye (Page 40, line 6 of the text) which had always felt advisable yet questionable. Simply to leave it at the duel being over was finally final enough.

Lastly, I would like to repeat that the alterations in manuscript form were usually made quickly, without much pause for reflection. Deeply involved in the writing, only nominally at the desk, transported almost physically away into the scene in mind, one does not need to pause much — the perceptions are so alerted that alternatives flicker through at computer speed, and hopefully the right one is selected in the instance of cutting.

But one matter I cannot deduce from the written pages: at what point did a day's work end, and another begin? I expect a handwriting expert could tell. I cannot. My only clue, and this is not a reliable one, is that when I have been writing for some time and the flow is fast, my letters tend to slope to the right.

All of which leads me to a further enquiry — into the material circumstances of the writing of this now much-filleted story.

5

In Case of Further Interest

Once I was asked to lecture on a literary subject of my choosing at Oxford. Uncertain of what might be of interest, I asked a don I knew what he thought about this. Without pause there came what seemed to be a remarkably undonnish answer. 'Tell them,' he said, 'how you do it yourself. When you write, where you sit, what you write with and so on. That's what they like to hear.' That happened on a station platform, a train drew in and bore him away without further explanation.

It seemed mean advice, rather in line with magazine stories of a theatrical star's homelife. But on consideration I saw he had a point. I found that I would be most interested to know how, say, favourites like Chekhov or Maupassant managed their working day. This would not hold up an exact pattern for me personally, since everyone's capacities and tastes are different, but it would provide an experienced structure against which I could judge my own way of going about things; and perhaps modulate it here, revolutionize it there. In any case, the temptation to spy on them at work fascinated.

We all know that books of value have been written in prison, or in other unpleasant circumstances. But their writers may have been of extraordinary tenacity; others of lesser will might have failed. One may thus suspect that it is not necessary to go to prison to write a book. What will now be discussed are the methods of a writer working in more ordinary circumstances.

I write at home, in a room reasonably secluded from the rest of the family. The windows look onto a large walled garden. In the summer I can step outside and carry on at a table in that garden. Visitors who penetrate this sanctuary squeal, 'How perfect!', 'What a wonderful place to write in!' and so on. Well, they are partly right. It is a lot more convenient and comfortable than many a corner I remember from the past. But they are wholly wrong in thinking that such quiet and seclusion means that the battle is won. It certainly does not.

Propitious terrain is welcome, but who invests it? A deficient creature. A mixed-up middle-aged kid made up of personal quirks and fears and insufficiencies, a baffling engine indeed.

As with travel, wherever you are, you bring your dear old self along too. There is quite a close analogy here with holidays — from brochure and armchair it seems that a completely new experience awaits us, once we are there we will be cleansed and different: but who do we bring along inside those bright new summer clothes? Somebody well known indeed, who will never change much.

In any case, seclusion is never complete. If you are removed from a regular rumble of traffic, then the irregular sounds of, say, bird-squawk intrude with amplified force; thrushes cut the brain with their pointed piping, pigeons thrash the bushes like thunder. Absurd? Doubly so, because it is exactly that precious quiet which makes it possible; and because the quiet makes the human animal keep a suspicious ear more alertly cocked. In the past I have written in an office full of ringing telephones, clattering typewriters, taffeta skirts — and I would say that finally the effect was about the same, though apparently poles apart, as in my present seclusion: as long as the noise is impersonal, it hardly matters — what matters is that you lose yourself in the work, and then you are somewhere else, and there are no sounds at all. So it is really in the first few minutes or quarter hour, when the page is blank and the mind applying but not applied, that the circumstances most affect you.

As a self-conscious person, I do a little tend to dramatise myself; even if very slightly, I hardly ever sit down to work without thinking in one part of me, Here I am, a writer, a novelist. And I suppose at this point a secluded desk in a booklined room with a garden window helps fulfil some adolescent dream. But, again, could it not be otherwise? In an office, seeing oneself as a writer battling with fearful odds? In corners of fire-stations, cold and lonely metallic corners, revelling in a sense of devoted sacrifice to the craft? Yes.

At another level I welcome an impersonal form of interruption. There is the famous instance of Somerset Maugham with his desk-view of garden and blue Mediterranean, and how he had that window bricked up because it interrupted him. I am the opposite. I like the company of such a view. Looking up at it now and again is like taking a refreshing drink. Does it drag me too fiercely back from fiction to reality? No. Only idly. It is on the whole impersonal, and I look at it in a kind of blurred, removed way. I have tried the opposite, turning my back to it. But then comes the question of the room, the walls: their day-after-dayness deadens — same old boring corners, walls, bookcases. A diurnal thereness about them makes me feel lonelier. Too easily they evoke the most lamentable of private emotions, self-pity. No, the garden-view is a kind of company.

Though it could as well be the view of a street. I enjoy very much, when abroad, writing in a chosen café. There one is in the company of the passing street, yet isolated, unapproachable. I always find myself going out to such a café in preference to the more apparent seclusion of my hotel room. Because of the company. A writer's life is a lonely one. This is perhaps its greatest burden. Though you may lose yourself, you are still on one level alone: when from time to time you come up for air, there is the silence and solitude ticking all around. I have often envied certain painters I know: inconceivably to me, they can go on working and talk to friends at the same time. Yet it is conceivable, I suppose, because their product is plastically revealed in front of them, solid and visible evidence of infinitely stronger pulling power than the writer's mechanical pages and mental screen. I well remember years when I worked in offices, and how much more comfortably the day passed — with its importances of telephones, secretaries, human contacts all along.

A long while ago, when I must have been eighteen or so, I learned an important lesson about the loneliness of writers. I was somewhere on holiday, and one of a group of friends happened, unusually then, to be a writer. This man never came down to the beach in the mornings with the rest of us. Instead, he got into a little car and went off inland to park somewhere in a country lane. In the little car was a little typewriter. I used to pity him. Yet one day, when he returned for lunch, I noticed a sense of achievement almost palpably emanating from him. And looked out for it on other days — and usually it was there. In fact, he was better off than any of us. He had created, he had achieved, he had used the time, his hat was all halo. I have never forgotten those emanations of virtue, they have helped enormously in deflating that vicious old self-pity.

So now the day begins with breakfast at eight-thirty, and a tootle in my mental little car downstairs to seclusion at about ten. Here an unassailably happy note is struck. Not one day passes without my being conscious and thankful that I do not have to face the commuter's journey, the wheels, the world, the facing of faces. Even if the weather is springlike and seductive, I prefer that safe descent of stairs to the walk to bus or station.

From breakfast to ten is not idle, there is the post, the paper. The paper I only skim. Ideally it should not be there, it should be as dispensable as it is on holiday in a foreign country: yet it is quite strongly seductive, one is curious of any major change overnight in the news, one has in any case a feeling of belonging to the world as evinced by all this daily print. However, I do not read it — except perhaps those quaint small happenings at the bottom of the page, food for fiction and usually stronger than fiction can pretend. This period of the day, with the mind hopefully freshened by sleep, is too valuable to be depressed by the world's deficiencies, the darker side that most easily makes news. The early evening is the time for this, the evening paper the satisfactory vehicle. Nevertheless, the morning headlines are a kind of company, and make for a sense of involvement at a safe remove.

Not so the post. This is plainly personal, and for a writer perhaps a greater pleasure than for others. Without an office, and segregated as far as possible from the telephone, it is his most solid contact with the world of his personal business. It contains his pay cheque, it contains new commissions; it contains also bills, but for the above reasons is still welcome and not, as others may complain, 'all bills'. Anyway, it has to be read: and of course curiosity could not relegate it to any other time of the day. Contemporaneously, there is the dear waking wife, and household plans for the day to be decided.

And so to bath, and the first bit of the day's real work: for that well-known, well-publicized inspiration-in-the-bath trick works as well today as ever. What is it about bathrooms — where even non-singers feel themselves free to sing? The freedom of lock and key? And more — the room is a liberator in itself, with few dust-gathering fabrics, much echo, and its function of cleansing and rebirth. Naked and locked, here is the first moment for the day's fresh mind to wander. And wander, with me, it daily does. I even start writing the first line or two, writing it on the air. On the way to bath from bedroom I always remember where I got to the day before, and that starts me off on today's work. In my bath this morning, so help us, I knew the point had come to mention baths in this book and the place in a writer's life of those watery, free-thinking, locked white cells of inspiration.

Downstairs, after a sniff outside at the weather, a vital sniff, for we metropolitans live as much by the weather as country folk, its pressures and the kind of light it sheds will have an effect on the whole day, even the day inside at a desk — downstairs then, and the actual writing day begins. From ten until one-thirty; when either lunch is ready, or I cut myself a sandwich. That one-thirty rather than one o'clock dates back from bachelor days, when I would often work on until two or three or whenever the thing inside stopped functioning. The extra half-hour above a usual one o'clock was as much as could reasonably be expected of the family.

Generally, these three-and-a-half hours are as much actual writing as I can manage. I have said earlier that, because of the tenseness of every nerve and muscle in body and mind, it is a more exhausting process than heavy manual labour; but it produces also, afterwards, a curiously refreshed state as well — there is the virtue of something attempted, something done (critical despondency will come later), the halo is cool as moussed snow, the whole organism as pleasantly exhausted as all those bodies in the towelled cool-rooms after their *saunat. (Saunat?* Naughty. I happened once to pick up this plural in Finland. Most people do not know it. It is a private preening, and an example of self-indulgence, like references to little-known painters or architects, which cries for cutting. If such matters are intended for information, this should be made politely explicit, not assumed with a darkly superior glow.)

And how many words a day? This is variable. A thousand on the very best days, and unusual. Five hundred would be perhaps an average. Sometimes it will be two hundred. Sometimes, on the worst days, a hundred — and these finally scored out.

The afternoon concerns itself with corrections of earlier work, correspondence, business of all kinds, proof-reading and perhaps any necessary research. All that, and planning for the next day — which can be done on a short walk.

But here again a happy note; before any proofs or walk or anything, twenty minutes on the sofa. If possible to sleep, behind a black eye-mask. Although it is pleasant, this is no precise self-indulgence: it is a calculated attempt to get back again that after-sleep freshness of the morning — to make two days of one. Often it works. In doing this, I follow in the somnolent tracks of many hard-pressed politicians and business man: I envy the man who can drop off at any moment for five, ten, fifteen minutes; he is usually extroverted, an unafraid type, very different from me, and this ability keeps him remarkably fresh and energetic for the next round. A conscious trick of the same kind was once taught me: sit back in a chair with a book suspended between the fingers and thumb of the right hand, relax, relax until you are completely gone and the book has fallen from your grasp. No sleep here, but a proved and absolute relaxation. It can work beautifully. And you do not have to be working at home to do it; come to think of it, this might well help the writer who has a daytime job, and who writes in the evening — five minutes at the end of his first working day might prove an ideal springboard for day number two.

I find that it is sometimes, though rarely, possible to put in an hour or two's further writing from about five o'clock to seven, depending on the nature of the work in hand. Seldom with fiction, more with articles, essays, a book of a general nature. It can be possible with fiction, too; but fiction is my first love, and I have a superstition against approaching it with a second wind. Pure creation of this kind, with no skeleton of fact to work on, makes a greater imaginative demand. There is a notion abroad that, *pace* the whitebeard acrobatics of Tolstoy, the writer of fiction ordinarily loses inspiration and powers of creative innovation as he grows past middle age. His best is done at a prime time. In case this might be true, prudence makes me relegate the same notion to the day's as well as the life's work.

Since the hardest part of writing, for me, is the prose — the constant search for a way to freshen it yet keep some framework of traditional cadence to get it all as pure as I can manage — since this is my weightiest grindstone. I try to read each day a few pages of a writer I admire. Chekhov, Bunin, Montherlant, Auden. The poets of the Greek anthology. People whose use of words, though in many cases in translation, comes through pure and trenchant. If man is still largely nine-tenths animal, I suspect that animal to be partly parrot.

The greater part of my own general reading is and has always been from translations, mostly from the Russians and French. I am not sure why. Plainly their view of life, though with the different writers in many ways dissimilar, attracted me. Possibly it was all begun early by some form of snobbery, a feeling that these European writers were more romantic, outrageous, sophisticated than those of cosy old England. Possibly it had simpler material beginnings — I know that in late adolescence I was given a number of volumes of the 'Great Short Stories of the World' type. Translations are said to lose a lot — they must do — but who knows how much they might gain? A translator is usually a scholar of sorts. His function may provide a further sieve for eradicating cliché and chattiness and over-richness from the original, formulating a more prosaic, in the best meaning of that word, product. One can only guess.

So the day goes on. Interrupted by few social engagements. There is none of the long literary pipe-smoking discussion which takes up, it seems from outside, so much of writers' lives. No vibrant café talk — there are no cafés. When English writers get together, they talk mostly about money. So that when I myself do go out and about, it is usually in some general circle, where life is in the raw. The writers I do know and count as friends would, I think, be friends in any case — because of much wider similarities in our attitudes and perceptions. There are, of course, literary parties given by publishers, useful for meeting editors. But I do not see how to get through the basic work and at the same time lead the complex social life one imagines of some leading writers: I do not expect they really manage this, I am sure I could not.

But it is obviously worthwhile to keep current with life by seeing a few plays and films, and by walking the ever-changing street. It would be absurd to stay in the ivory tower — that is a contrivance to go back to from somewhere else. But here we come to a newish problem — the ivory tower is no longer inhabited only by a family and books of your own selection, but also by any number of moving, talking and highly-coloured visiting faces. Television, in fact. Most families have one, as most families have the electric light. Yet both are optional. One is not commanded to turn the television on. But it is mighty seductive. For a writer, doubly so — it is a relief, though perhaps false, for eyes wearied by too much print; and it is, or seems to be, informative. It has become so much part of life that sometimes one wonders how certain evenings were passed without it. Did one actually talk? Did one read? Did one potter? The too-enclosed writer may find himself in much the same situation as a very old person — here is life on a plate to be lived vicariously. Dangerous, indeed.

And I do find with television one other particular danger to the writer's technique. It is a matter of reference. Television has such an intimate, switch-on-and-off presence that all about it has a peculiarly ephemeral value. Whereas previously pieces of information, or moments of drama, or slices of life could be nailed down in memory by certain books read, plays or films seen, public places visited — here there is no material occasion to frame experience in the memory. It all comes out of the air, vanishes into air. I am constantly wondering where I read this, or saw that. No reference occurs, and no exact reference means that you do not carry a criticism with you of your source of information. Loosely, it is too easily believed. The critical abilities become blurred. Its effects are almost alcoholic.

Returning to the writing of the particular story under discussion, I have looked back in my diaries and tried to find the particular circumstances under which it was written. No work is done in a vacuum. There is past work creeping up on you in various proof form, there is the slow incubation of future plans. Unfortunately I do not keep an exact record of when a story was begun and finished. However, I can pin this one down to the autumn of 1961, say from September to the hiatus of Christmas. The summer holiday, spent in a Portuguese heat-wave, was over. During that Portuguese August, I spent part of the time finalizing proofs of a novel, part travelling a bit about Portugal for an article to be written on return, and part sheltering from the heat by the open door of a refrigerator — nursing both a broken rib and a stomach attack which necessitated occasional vomiting which broke the rib again. So the diary of September lst, the day of return, says just: 'Rest'.

But I know from the finishing stages of that novel that a period of doing shorter work had begun. This is always so with me and in this case I had these commissions to write about places, Gotland and the Portuguese atmospheres and landscapes. So-called travel-writing had been for several years a financial standby. I had determined to avoid the regular job which most writers have to take now to be able to live. But I had good free-lance connections with American and other magazines: travelling and writing for them took up about three months of the year, leaving the rest free for the writing of fiction.

This travel journalism was beneficial in many ways: it provided that vital basic income, it got me away to foreign places free, and it had a therapeutic writing value in that it satisfied much of my painter *manqué's* need for close visual description, too much of which was liable to infect my fictional work. Also, I took more trouble with the prose of these pieces than was perhaps necessary for the magazines where they were published; this came both from an inherent interest in words, and also because I knew that afterwards I could bind the articles together into an acceptable volume of travel essays. It was thus somewhere about the time of writing of these travel pieces, and possibly of other short stories, that *No Smoking on the Apron* was written. Also, for the future, silver-lined clouds were mounting. There was a move on, with a theatrical director and a composer, for me to write the libretto of a musical play — one of those distinct changes which from time to time tempt an author. So there was very little vacuum about.

But was there a 'writer's block' about too? If there was, this horrid plague was not noted in my diary. By good fortune, I seldom suffer so. But when it comes, it is painful indeed. It is like those days we all know when nothing seems worth doing — when books are picked up and put down, plans made and rejected, and even a short walk seems worthless. Such days, notable in childhood, follow us into adult life — and with the writer and his profession, occasionally stretch into weeks of dreadful drought. A low feeling; nothing seems worth writing about, the whole process of letters useless. There seems to be no immediate cure for it but to buzz off to new scenes, refreshment. Yet the very accidie, the torpor prevents such buzzing. What would be the use? says the malevolent and shrunken mind. Then, one wonderful day, it all passes as if it had never been. It is inconceivable that it could have been. Life seems suddenly far, far too short for everything that yells to be put into words. The mania is on again, the depression past.

One of these attacks may or may not have come on that autumn. In my case, since it passes, it is unimportant. So the weeks would have gone on with the aforesaid daily work, and various comings and goings of a business nature — American editors arrive in London and go, ditto my Portuguese publisher, a Japanese bookseller, and so on; and other comings and goings of a domestic kind — the appearance and disappearance of *au pair* girls, gardeners and builders — and one matter I have hitherto not mentioned, the garden itself. With me, a garden presence has always been close to the writing day. When I took the plunge and chanced my hand as a full-time free-lance writer, at a time when I had little money at all, my very inexpensive damp basement flat had a blessed garden attached. Thus, years afterwards, the first house I was able to afford had a garden — intentionally this time. And so on to my present house.

Not only is a garden company, as I have already said, but it also makes demands. These are sometimes of a nuisance nature — digging, weeding, cutting, clearing. However, for a sedentary creature who refuses the time for organized exercise, it commands attention and bending and muscle for short periods. It is a mild therapy in itself. And I also subscribe to the old dictum that man lives at best in some way close to the earth. Earth, trees, leaves do him good. The seasons are sniffed, plant growth is created, a slow sense of real time experienced. An obvious and salutary situation, particularly for the metropolitan citizen. If no garden, then a window box should be essential for writers, if one can employ such a general term as 'writers' for such a very various breed.

This brings up a final question, put I imagine mostly by the young: how do I get the house and garden? The answer, I am afraid, will sound like preaching: for the answer is simply save, save, save. When I first became a full-time writer, rather late in the day at thirty, I had one book published, one commissioned book worth £250 to write (but over a year and a half to do it in), a few unreliable magazine contacts for articles, a few low-paying literary magazine contacts for short stories, and £113 in the bank. This was in 1945. It stood out a mile – the only way out was to save. Only in this way could one buy the leisure to write.

A lot of writers do live, it is true, from hand to mouth: one moment flush, the next broke. It seemed to me that this would make for too anxious a life. So I took the other way and dispensed with a lot of luxuries and amusements, so that I could save for the future. I cannot say it was difficult, they seemed unimportant compared with the great pleasure, even the necessity, of writing. Still today I find about me the remnant habits of these economies: I still shave with toilet soap, still have no flannel, still wear a working shirt far too long.

These economies have worked well. They have inculcated an inclination to enjoy spending money only when it brings a worthwhile return, not to waste it. This does not mean parsimony, it includes good food and wine; but it does not include taking a taxi when there is time for a bus with a view, or a short walk. Over the years now, together with regular working hours, this has built up a provident income. I began publishing at a lucky time, at the end of the war and start of the peace, when people read largely because there was not so much organized amusement, not so many household gadgets to play with, and above all no television. (Television and its semination of knowledge may have led to greater readership for more of that knowledge in unlikely quarters; but on the other hand, it has taken away advertising revenue from magazines, newspapers, and hence slimmed or closed up many a writer's outlet.)

So in those days it was easier for a writer to establish himself than today. I managed to achieve a *succès d'estime*, something of a name, which holds me in good stead but does not necessarily mean best-selling. So I repeat that the only way out is to save, save, save. Have a splash; but then start saving again.

Meanwhile, the routine of writing fiction year after year can, and perhaps must, be varied. It is only human. It is the reason, for instance, for this present study.

6
Happily Ever After

Finally, a word about the progress of *No Smoking on the Apron*. It was first published in *London Magazine*. It was reprinted five years later in *Argosy*. It formed part of a collected volume of my short stories called *The Ulcerated Milkman*. It has been translated for magazines in Sweden and Holland.

Its life is young yet. At random I have looked at the record of that first story I had published in *Horizon*: there have since been certainly twenty-three different printings or broadcasts, probably more. And at random another — *The Vertical Ladder* has had twenty-six different publications across the world, and on the way has provided the title story for a book of my stories specially selected for upper schools and universities. Other stories have for one reason or another not done so well. A short story may not strike oil like a novel, but nevertheless it can make a useful little silver mine.